SPIRAL

by

Christopher Turco

For fellow artist and dreamer
Aurora O'Brien
A true muse and good friend.

© 2017 Christopher Turco, All Rights reserved.
Cover Art by Aurora O'Brien
Visit Aurora at: www.patreon.com/Aurorart
Visit my Patreon at: www.patreon.com/MistahTurco

"My memories have sharp teeth tonight. Perhaps the boundaries of our character are formed by outlines of regret."

- Observation of Bennel Wehns, Morosian Contemplator

It wasn't just Gress the Innkeeper's life that changed the day the elf came to Spiral. But he was the first to guess at the implications.

He would not describe himself as a bright man. He would instead go on about the virtues of being humble and why practicality mattered. This last part was a half truth: Though Gress kept an immaculate Inn and was renowned for the quality of his lodgings, he wasn't very practical about taking care of himself. Success had thickened him all over, and as gray intruders sprouted in his dark beard, he found more and more reason to slow down. Where once he walked, he lumbered, and where he once looked people in the eye, he averted his gaze.

He was situated at the outermost edge of Spiral, where tourists frequently came in from around the continent. His lodgings where popular among those applying for a tourist permit, with a view across the white marble of the Old City and on the other side, a view of the brown walled Lesser Reaches. He had been at that perch now for seventeen years, rarely venturing far, and spending his earnings on what delights he could find at a discount.

If Gress were to look inward, he'd admit that the truth was, he was a man without direction or hope. He daydreamed not at all, and often took his amusement from quietly judging the customers who breezed in and out on any given day. He had little appetite for music or art, and found his eye rarely wandering to women. He existed as a passionless thing, an automaton that simply provided a service with some menial mental clarity thrown in as an extra. He was a simple enough man that this served well enough for his own sake.

All of this changed when she came through the door. A quiet had settled on the street, which he distantly thought as odd because the Nightsong was still two hours off. Then the door creaked open. A hooded figure entered, and the door swung shut.

Gress simply watched the entering figure, noting the grace of her movements and the hint of her build beneath the cloak, eyes wide.

She lowered her hood. There she stood, the most beautiful living thing he'd ever seen. She had a mane of long black hair that emerged from her hood in teasing ebon streaks before she'd lowered it. Her face had flawless symmetry, the most perfectly beautiful bone structure he could ever imagine, even with his limited powers of the mind. She had crystal blue eyes with black motes around the iris that almost looked like extra pupils and flawless pale skin. Her ears tapered to a definitive point.

Her robes parted as she approached him, revealing an outfit of sky blue elven silk weaving around her body. There was gold detail over darker blue at the hips in interlocking patterns that he guessed had some elven significance.

However, It was the collection of sapphires embedded into her flesh just below the neck, arrayed across her sternum and collar bones that he fixated on. There was one large one over her heart, two smaller ones flanking that, and two much smaller ones beneath each of those. There were three coin sized sapphires embedded in the backs of her hands in a triangle pattern.

He blinked several times. He felt a new attention on him, the way someone feels when they walk out of a cold room into sunlight. This was a creature beyond his imagination, and her presence here was a mounting impossibility that threatened the stasis of his day to day life with the notion of real difference. His mind buckled inwardly at the pressure. After all, no elf had come to Spiral in a century, at least. But here she was, and her dazzling power began to rearrange the walls of his mind with her sheer presence.

In a voice as even and smooth as her garments, she told him

casually, "I need a room for at least a week, and I need to know how to get a tourist permit for the Old City."

He stumbled off his stool, suddenly a traitor beneath his numb legs, and nodded. A fierce warmth took to his cheeks, but if she noticed, she said nothing. She stared at him with the total detachment of a higher life form, but absent judgment or cruelty.

That realization humiliated him. In one moment, he felt self-conscious of all the mean things he thought of visitors past, and and realized how small and unjust a thing he really was to be so quick on such matters. He couldn't look her in the eye. Her absence of judgment somehow judged him.

He pushed the ledger toward her and cleared his throat, eyes on her hands as she rested them on the counter top. "It's five silver per night. Your room will be up the stairs and second door on the right."

She probably nodded. He didn't know. He watched her hands take a quill from the mostly empty ink pot and sign the ledger. She took her time doing it, signing her name as a work of art with flourish and embellishment. *Anathea.*

"No last name?" he asked, voice foreign in his throat.

"None worth mentioning at this point," she said. "Will you assist me with my things?"

He came around the counter without a word and wished he'd lit the incense in the lobby. He shouldered two large sacks – where had they come from? Did she bring them in? Did she drag them, set them down at the door? He had been so distracted, so disarmed. What else could he fail to notice?

Shame crept on him in a second wave, and he realized how little of the world he must have seen. How little of it he had participated in over forty years, working first here as a youth and taking it over when his father passed. His head spun as his limited means struggled to consider what wonders laid upon the horizon, where the sun set and the clouds strolled with such abandon every day of his life.

Her room was a spacious one, with a purple, hand woven carpet featuring the symbol of Spiral, a butterfly, in gold. The floor and walls were polished wood, and two walls had bookcases featuring local classics for the lodger's pleasure. There was a twin bed with purple covers edged in gold, and a nightstand to each side. One had an incense burner with a candle, flint and stone, while the other had a large pitcher of water and two glasses.

"This seems quite generous for five silver," she said. "I'll be happy to stay here. I wonder if I might impose, though. I don't know what your policy is, but I see I've attracted much attention on the streets. Could you please ensure I'm not disturbed? I can pay extra."

"Well, you're the first elf to come to Spiral in decades," he answered her. "No one's ever seen your like in this generation, maybe longer. The people out there are...curious."

"I'm not here to brook curiosity, unfortunately. Tell me, have you heard of a hero named Buron Hale?"

"We all know the story of Buron Hale here. How he lost his loved ones when Thurach attacked the city and set out to even the score, we all know the stories. There are poems and ballads about him now, and a play or two that's regularly performed. In fifty years, no one's forgotten him."

"In fifty years, neither have I," she said, and her eyes were suddenly sad. Her entire face pouted, and he swore he'd never seen a face so expressive before. "I've come here to touch his legacy."

"Pardon the question, I hope, but what do the elves know of Buron Hale? He's a human hero."

"You'd find he's an elven hero as well. What if I told you I had met him, those fifty years back? When a dragon had taken us both prisoner?"

Gress fluttered his eyes and stammered. "That's...very interesting. Really. I mean, you don't look old enough, pardon me saying so."

"Elves live well past your lifespan and our youth extends likewise. I'm ninety-one years old, still a new thing in the world to my people. I'll look young yet for another century before I start showing age. Not that an extended lifespan is a blessing. If all you hear are echoes of loss and pain, believe me, the promise of years fanning out into the distance with nothing but your wounds to keep you hardly seems like good news."

"You say you were taken by a dragon. You say you knew Buron. There have been rumors of this sort of thing. People have described a lady elf in the story as well. You say this is you?"

"Those stories came from the elven lands. My people wanted to authenticate my story when I showed up unharmed after being missing for some time. Imagine their shock when my claims turned out to be true. But that's all I want to say of it for now, do forgive me. I've come here to visit an old ghost in particular, not to be pursued by all of them."

"Your wish, my lady. Forgive my intrusion. I'll leave you to get acquainted with your surroundings. The balcony is behind that purple set of curtains there. The double doors are locked but you can come and go there without a key."

"Thank you for your kindness. I'll speak of you fondly."

She nodded once more and took to lighting the incense. He retreated from the room and shut it behind her. The keys had been left on a hook next to the door on the inside of her room, as was his standard procedure.

He slowly walked down the stairs, then sat at his stool with a plop. He was a stranger in his own skin. His life was an alien thing to him now. How misunderstood. How wasted. How small.

Over the next five minutes, he resolved to collect his fortunes, sell the Inn, and leave Spiral. To go...anywhere. East. West. Over the mountains. He had more than enough to afford that. To see *things*. To participate in *life*. While he was still able to, even in his less than healthy form.

Gress had always been a stranger to pure inspiration.

Anathea stood out on her balcony with her hood pulled up. The people pointed and stared. She stepped back from the balcony and studied the fading glow in the sky.

She couldn't help her curiosity. This was *his* city, the fabled Spiral. A city she'd never have thought about if not for her momentary friendship with Buron Hale, a hero who had saved her from certain death at the cost of his own life. For decades, she had dreamed of seeing this place in person. She devoured any trivia or traveler's story she could find on the largest and greatest of human cities.

And now, here she was, standing on a balcony and breathing the cool Fall air of a giant metropolis. The narrow street below was busy with foot traffic, and a pair of constables clad in enameled armor moving people on so they wouldn't gawk long. There were metal bars curling across the outside of each building, including her own, some with leather wrappings around them.

This, she knew, was the favorite travel system of the small and strange gliphids. They stood three feet tall at best and possessed an agility humans could never understand. They often scurried about those frameworks as a courtesy to the human traffic below. She knew they were purple skinned with large, ink black eyes and particularly long, pointed ears. They had four vocal chords, she'd been told, and they could mimic most sounds or sing quartets by themselves.

She smiled in spite of her brooding mood. This was just one of Spiral's wonders. Tomorrow, after she rested and had a good breakfast, she would take to the streets and sort out the world around her. Anathea was anxious to touch the soul of Buron Hale, even indirectly. Some lingering impression of him within her psyche wanted to touch Spiral again as well.

As Anathea left the balcony, she was oblivious to an ordinary man in his late twenties watching her with awe from the streets below, a slightly unkempt fellow who had not the best frame or a lantern jaw, but whose sincere eyes were wide with astonishment.

Beside him, invisible to all living things in Spiral, the Goddess Anastasia hovered above the scene on golden wings. Eyes glittering with emotion, she smiled. *Oh, whatever will happen next?*

"The religion of Anastasia the Muse is a curious thing. It holds passion, creativity and inspiration more dear than any other mundane element. It stresses a need for wisdom, education and expression rather than subversion, dominance or control. It is an outsider religion at best, but against all odds, it has flourished in the heart of Spiral. Even the non-artists hold the Muse beloved. Those that disagree with her religion, called the Mindful, argue that it's a religion of decadence and distraction. The children of the Muse insist there is nothing finer."

- **Official report Anastasia's religion (Called "Stasism")**

to the court of King Ronmacharte II

Anastasia the Muse hovered over the plaza with her wings outstretched, watching the scene below her with solid gold eyes. No mortal eye could see her, for she did not wish it. Anyone she permitted to would have seen a woman of unsurpassed beauty looking down upon them, with a mane of curly auburn hair stirring in the wind and a dress made of living rose petal clinging to her perfect form.

Her eyes followed one human in particular as he wound his way through the crowd. She flexed her wings and descended slowly, landing next to him without a sound. She took up a stride alongside him. The twelve foot tall Muse had no trouble keeping pace with this mortal who barely came up to her waist.

"Mortals are stuck with talking to each other's heads," she said to him in a honey-sweet voice. "I'm going to talk to your heart instead and trust that it'll hear me. That's my favorite place to be heard, as you must well know. You're a frequent visitor to my temple so I'm sure you know all about me."

Anastasia plucked a ring-coin off a leather strap as a wealthy man passed by. The man had forgone the protective flap concealing his row of ring-coins from view, eager to display his wealth to the ladies. Anastasia plucked it free from the leather strap holding them as though it had been made of air. She flicked it into the air with her fingers and caught it again like a toy.

"Right now, your heart is beating so fast. I can hear it. I can feel it. It's the best kind of heartbeat, the kind quickened by the visage of something beautiful. It beats so passionately, even my words may be lost in their chambers. But I can forgive that, because let's face it, kiddo. Passion's my middle name." She chewed her lip. "Well, maybe not. 'Anastasia Passion the Muse.' Nevermind. Forget I said it."

She held the ring-coin in her hand and snapped her fingers. It appeared on the leather strap of a fruit salesman the two of them passed on the street. One of his golden apples appeared in her hand. She took a slow bite.

"I love the apples in this world, you know that? But back to business. You're inflamed for that elf you saw. I know this feeling well and it's my favorite feeling in any reality I've known. The thundering heart, the flushed cheeks, the fevered dreams. That sunburst of hope that comes from seeing that someone that no one else could ever be.

"You've seen the sun crest the mountains for the first time in looking into those blue eyes of hers. You've breathed fresh air for the first time in months by hearing her speak. You never knew an angel until you saw it hiding in the subtle lines of her form, compelling your thoughts with newfound divinity. You're one step away from love itself in the purest form it can know. Forget the falling part; you're in mid-air right now and going straight down into that velvet embrace."

The Muse sighed and bit the apple again, Her audience continued to weave through the crowd, head bent, legs fast, a leather folder of his poetry under one arm. He shouldered a man aside, who turned to shout at this trespass until Anastasia's fingertips glanced his forehead. The man simply turned and walked away.

"Oh, yes. There's all that frustration, too. Let's not gloss over that tension. Your want is in scale to your anxiety. Will she be yours? Could she be? How possible is it? Dare you dream? Will you curse yourself for laying eyes on someone part of you knows you'll never have, or will you listen to that attraction blooming in such force instead, trusting that maybe this time, things will different and you'll feel her arms around your body at night?"

Another bite of the apple. "Listen, you. Love is going to be dark and it's going to be bright. It will bring out the best of you and it can bring out the worst in you. Don't go hog wild trying to analyze every little thing about it; it's meant to be mad and beyond scrutiny. You can't put scientific method to love and keep the most vital aspects of that magic alive.

"Your only role right now is to decide how it moves you and to what end. You'll wonder if you can ever live without her, but in all that dreamy eyed fantasizing you're doing, do you really know if you can live with her? So many connections start with fantasy. Then reality intrudes and the difference in the sum comes due. Don't write a script around her behavior before you know her. I make no promises."

He stopped beside a trash can on a street corner. Anastasia stopped beside him. He reached into his folder and pulled out his collection of poetry.

Anastasia's eyes widened. "Don't you dare, now. Think twice! Nothing affronts me like the destruction of a heartfelt work. Think it over! Who cares what your friend said about it? I'd rather see bad poetry then no poetry at all. He can't claim to know my mind on such things. Don't let an insult with my name carelessly slung around unseat your conviction. Go lay that upon my altar and let the muses take it. If you would really part with your words, I prefer it be done that way."

The poet lowered his hand, then stuffed the poetry back into his folder. Anastasia smiled.

"That's a good lad. For the record, you might stand a bit of improvement, but I've been offered far worse and been begged for far more in return. Here you are, swooning over that elf, drunk in head and pants alike, let's be honest, but you know what? You're not asking me to grant her to you like every other idiot on that street. I noticed that. I appreciated it."

He turned on one heel, eyes narrow and heaved along his course by a heavy sigh. Anastasia walked beside him again. "You see, I can't take a direct hand in this world. Don't worry about why, it's a long story between me and the other Amaranthines. How many poets and artists and composers shower my altar with their belabored works, begging me to grant them the object of their affection in return.

"Do you know why I don't? Because it insults me. They would expect me to bend a man or woman's heart against its nature to please them, just for paying what they think is a fair price in ink and paper. Love must be a choice. It must be its own thing and it has the greatest of all the power it represents when it occurs naturally. I won't whore out some stranger for some middling bit of verse or half-baked symphony. How would that be fair to anyone?"

They crossed an intersection where flowers hung from the four posts bracketing the meeting of the streets. They had gone without water for two days and were about to shed their petals until Anastasia blew them a kiss. They blossomed again in full and the scent drifted down onto the intersection with a convenient stir of the wind.

"One hundred and twenty-six people saw Anathea on that balcony alongside you. What can I tell you about that? I can read hearts at a glance. Half a dozen men resented their wives. Thirty women even hated the elf on the spot. More than enough of the crowd coveted her, members of both sexes measuring their wants to their ambition for her and wondering how they could scheme the two to meet. Seven other artists looked upon her and immediately begged for my favor in wooing her, mainly for lust than for love in any shape.

"And then there was you: The poet, the secret gentleman scribbling poetry at that cafe table. You looked up at her and were as stirred by her majesty as all the rest, but you did not beg me for her gifts. You did not bargain with me in offering to grant her to you. You did not lust out of kind and forsake any other virtue she held."

Anastasia smiled and brushed aside his hair, taking a last bite of her apple. "You swooned in heartfelt awe and you shed a tear. You wept to behold her because you saw her as the most beautiful thing that ever lived, male or female or whatever. You were moved down to your bones. Your very reality turned inside out just to see her there, leaning on the rails of that Inn and looking out across the city of Spiral with such curiosity. Don't you usually hum your favorite Nightsongs as you walk? Here you are in silence as you go, the music in your heart swelling to provide you a tune in quiet. You know you feel love when you can walk in total silence and hear music enough to please anyone coming from the depths of your own thoughts."

He turned a corner and Anastasia tossed the apple over her shoulder and into a garbage can. It landed dead center even though she didn't bother to look. The Temple of the Muse was ahead, a multistory building with a long courtyard garden before it. The garden was lined with hand carved marble statues in various elegant dance poses, all of them nude and precisely detailed. Anastasia followed her charge into the two story tall double doors of the building, passing sculpted pillars on the front porch designed to resemble rising spirals. There were many entrances around the building that led to the main hall, but she always preferred the lavish main path.

She paused inside the doors and breathed in the aroma of flowers and incense surrounding her. "Gods, I love this place. They really got it right, you know. I've been worshipped in other realities under other names, you realize, but this temple in particular is probably my favorite."

He passed the scantily clad men and women that served as Anastasia's muses - the Court of the Muse, as they were known - and went to the central chamber to view the twenty foot statue of Anastasia herself. It was easy business for her subject to ignore the scantily clad, well muscled young men and women, but he looked upward at Anastasia's statue without hesitation..

It was a precise rendition of the Muse in stone, anatomically perfect and painstakingly painted to look entirely alive. Faux hair was embedded in the statue's scalp, and the statue was dressed in a revealing dress of purple silk.

"Oh, I love that look," Anastasia muttered. "Slit up both sides for the legs and wide open from the waist up to show everything off. I even like the bandeau top but I think it needs to be a lot smaller, don't you?" She snapped her fingers and her dress shifted into the modification of the statue's outfit that she had described. "Very cozy. I'm keeping the living rose petal thing, though. It's entirely too comfortable.

"Meanwhile: what are you going to do, oh poet mine? Live up to my faith this last little while, please. Don't beg me for the elf. Don't offer me anything for her or I'll lose all faith in you. I've been kind enough to stay out of your thoughts this far because the sheer feeling coming off of you is intoxicating enough. Don't lose my esteem with some lecherous bargain."

The other penitent artists laid their offerings at Anastasia's altar, gently lowering them before her stone feet before praying and moving on. The poet's turn came next. He knelt before her statue and placed one hand over his heart, the other on his forehead. The typical position for a prayer to the Muse.

Anastasia held her breath and listened.

"Anastasia," he whispered, "Avatar of creation, scion of beauty, source of passion."

He paused.

She chewed her lip. "Yes? Come on? I'm right here listening, for the Travellers' sake."

"Forgive me for being too imperfect to love."

He rose, dropped two ring-coins into a cup held by one of the Courtiers, and made for the door.

Anastasia watched him, open mouthed. She slapped a palm to her face. "Too imperfect? That's it?" She blurted out. "Too imperfect to love? Really? You, the one man who looked upon that elf with a song in his heart instead of the throb of his loins or the seething of the insecure? You, the one man that saw light over mere lust. You're too imperfect to love? What melodramatic self-loathing is this?"

She shifted through space to stand before him. He stopped in place, but had no idea necessarily why. Anastasia leaned in and whispered to him.

"Listen. I can never promise anyone's heart to you. We've covered that little detail already. I will do this for you, though. Carry forth in good faith with her and I'll not only see that you two at least meet face to face, but you may yet receive the greatest gift she can offer you. If, if, if you continue in good faith. If you earn it. I won't have you, of all people, give up hope so quickly, however. Spiral is my city, friend. You have my blessing in this so long as your purpose with her is selfless."

She flicked a wing and caught the feather that dislodged. She tucked into his tunic beside his poetry. "Try writing with that. You'll find my feather makes a wonderful quill. You'll remember buying it here at the temple at the shop on the way out. Deep down inside, though, you'll know it's my badge of honor. Go forth and make poetry in the world."

Anastasia stepped aside. She watched the poet sigh again, frustrated at his own odd behavior, and then march for the door. Anastasia stayed behind and watched him exit.

"Dark powers will be marshaling against her soon. Envy breeds discontent and not only among the peasantry. Other eyes are already measuring their gain from her, my dear poet. She'll need a friend in this city, a friend with unique connections and abilities like you. Human nature must chart its own course, so I can't intervene. As my chosen in this matter, though, you certainly can.

"It's good that your name is Brace. I'll take that as a pleasant accident of fate, yet be aware, Brace the Poet, Brace the Gentleman: Love seldom blooms without an offering of tragedy to nourish it. I feel something coming in the distance already. Your time may yet come when you have to be strong."

"He took her into his arms like a man who wanted to. His face, furry as a fuzzymug, parted with an airy sigh and he said to her, "You are the beer of my soul. I could drink your face. I could---"

- (Unfinished work by Brace Galter, ended abruptly, scratched out, crumpled up and thrown into the garbage).

Brace slouched over a round wooden table at the Happy Harpy tavern, staring into his drink. He tapped the wooden mug against the table, staring himself cross-eyed at the shifting patterns of the fluid inside.

A man his age with a mane of blonde hair dropped his gold enameled gauntlets onto the table. Each was the length of his forearm and had a large amber gem that would rest against the back of his hand.

Brace ignored him. The man cleared his throat twice. He wore armor of the same make as the gauntlets, with an even larger amber gem over his heart.

"I'm here," he said.

"Yes, you are," Brace answered. He swirled his drink around some more.

"Who are you kidding? Why are you drinking here?"

"To forget my troubles, Ander."

"But you don't drink. Have you ever been drunk in your life?"

"I can have the satisfaction carbonation and sweet flavors can bring, can't I?" He brushed the mug aside. "Go ahead, ruin my somber mood."

"With pleasure. You need out of that 'creator' depression of yours, anyway."

"I suppose unwelcome tidings are the cure."

"What's got you so eaten up this time? Did they not like your poetry at the Temple of the Muse again?"

"You say that so casually."

"Well, what is it?"

Brace sighed. "I saw the most beautiful woman in history today."

Silence reigned for a few moments.

"I thought artists types were all about that," Ander said. He signaled a bar maid to bring him a drink.

"It's the despair of seeing something I can never comprehend," Brace told him. "I can't find words to describe who I saw. I've never seen a beauty so arresting, so radiant, so overwhelmingly perfect to behold. Everything about her, literally everything, was flawless. She stood out against the tide of flesh washing across Spiral's street like a glittering sapphire in the desert sun."

"Sounds like you're describing her just fine." Ander tipped the barmaid and took along sip from his mug. "Good thing they know me here. I don't have to order."

"You don't get it. I've spent my life obsessing over words and verse. I've found the moment where words *fail*. That's sort of a big deal. That's like learning your religion is a lie or everything you ever treasured about someone was total falsehood. It's a breach of my deepest beliefs."

"She's an insult to your vanity, then."

Brace sat up straight. "She is not! What? An insult to my vanity?"

"You saw something you can't explain with your vaunted art of words and you're taking it poorly." Another sip.

"You wouldn't snicker at me if you saw her. Everyone on the street was at a dead stop. One glance at an elf and the world grinds to a halt."

Ander stopped cold. The mug was suspended just in front of his mouth. "An elf?"

"Yeah, an elf. I warrant she was an elf. She had the ears. Sort of an elf thing."

"There's an elf in Spiral. Seriously?"

Brace rested his face on one hand and slouched at the table. "E-l-f. You getting it now?"

Ander thought it over, shrugged and said, "Nope."

Brace let his forehead tap the table. He patted the table with his hands in a gesture of surrender.

"I'm not quite the romantic you are, I guess." Ander resumed sipping.

"I know. You have the vocabulary the Spiral Guard is afforded for his job, which is a step above animal grunting."

"That's mean, thank you very much. I'm slightly better than grunts on most days. I'm feeling downright outgoing right now."

"To return to the topic, what artist can survive encountering something that shakes their creative core to their bones? My mission in life, much as you like to berate it and mock it, is capturing the beauty of the world, any way I can. I believe in that. Words are my tool. What do you do when words fail? How do survive finding something or someone beyond your best description?"

"I'd describe her as an elf with a case of the hots." He finished the bottom of his mug and signaled the barmaid for more.

"And that, dear friend, is why you and I talk nothing on the matters of love and beauty. The topic escapes you. Doesn't it occur to you that lavishing wordplay on her is more worthy than just 'an Elf with the hots?' Doesn't she deserve real tribute?"

"What do you consider real tribute to be? Writing her a book?"

"It would be a start. It would be more than just a pile of words! For a beauty like that I'd need to write a few books, I think."

Ander shrugged and thanked the barmaid, then froze up. He stiffened and turns toward Brace fully, casting sidelong glances across the room.

"What the Shei'os is it, Ander?"

Ander arched an eyebrow and nodded to the side. "She's here. Talais Runholde."

Brace craned his neck to see before Ander gently pushed his cheek to face him again. "Don't look!" Ander hissed. "Come on, don't give me away."

Brace looked with greater subtlety. There she was, a statuesque woman with a mane of brown hair, wearing the same armor Ander wore.

"So that's her, huh? The great love of your life?"

"The love of my life, the beat of my loins, the empty in my heart."

"'The beat of your loins?' Really? Maybe you're a writer deep down."

"Don't condescend to me. This is serious! I've been dying to say something to her for weeks. This is the first time I've met her outside work! Is she with anyone? Who is she talking to? Is there a guy around her?"

"Lots of guys around her being that it's a tavern. Other than that, looks like she's just having a drink."

Ander blushed, then paled. Brace stared wide eyed at his

circulatory panic. "It's the perfect time. I can do this. I can finally say something. What do I say? You're the writer! Tell me something clever! Something poetry! C'mon!"

"Haven't we just discussed the limits of my language?"

"She's not an elf, we're fine! C'mon! Help me out! I'll buy two rounds of whatever flimsy drink you're sucking down. Give me something good."

"Well, steer away from 'guardswoman with the hots."

Ander nodded. Brace sighed. "Fine," he said, and took out his notebook. He uncapped a small bottle of ink and pulled the golden quill from a leather folder of quills, all of this things he had kept beside his stool. He jotted quickly and put a flourish on the final words before handed the paper to Ander.

The guardsman read the passage, then slowly looked up at Brace with an arched eyebrow.

"Are...you....serious?"

"You wanted something poetic. I promise that will get her attention. Say it under your breath a few times and then go try it out."

"You're totally serious?"

"Do I not know the words that win a woman's heart?"

"No. Probably not. Like you said, we were over that just now."

Brace rolled his eyes. "Ye of little faith. Trust the writer. Scoot. Try it."

Ander blushed again, then stood up and approached the bar where Talais was tipping back mugs. He greeted her with obvious shyness.

Brace pulled out a copper watch, flipped open the lid, and watched the second hand cycle around.

He watched Talais stare at Ander with horror, and Ander making for the door with his eyes on the floor. Talais looked at Brace. He started counting.

Talais wandered over to Brace's table. "I saw Ander drinking with you. What just happened?"

"Poor guy just put his foot in his mouth, eh? Sorry about that. Look, he's been absolutely dying to say something to impress you for ages now. He's talked me up and down about how much he admires your intelligence and your strength. He's told me, no lie, you practically redefine the Spiral Guard. He's sort of in a state of amazement over you."

Talais blinked. "Really?"

"He is. He snaked something I was working on when I was leaning over and putting my quill keeper down. He probably hoped he could sound funny and urbane when he broached the subject. He does try to lead in with a laugh. Some of the most charming people do. Can I ask which quote he swiped from my notebook?"

She shifted back and forth on her feet. "'Your brain is a like a big, wrinkled breast that makes me want to mentally reach through your skull and grope with my mind fingers.'"

Brace winced. "Oh, by the Muse. That's for a comedy play I'm writing. So, he was trying to lead in with a joke, after all. He was probably so shy with you he botched the delivery up and down the block. In the play I'm using it for someone who's hitting on a brainy barmaid, so I jotted it down when it came to me. Dreadfully sorry. Damn, he's never going to forgive me for that! I'm sorry if inspired him to make a bad impression on you."

"Oh, no, I'm so sorry. He's a good man, he really is. Truth told, I've...noticed him before. He's an excellent guardsman. He has real compassion for the people. Really, a credit to the field."

"Look, this has all been a big mistake and I'm overwhelmed with apology for it. If I know him, he'll be at that fountain outside pounding on the sides of his head with his fists. Maybe you can take his gauntlets back to him and sort of pave things over? I'd happily buy you both a drink for the confusion. I assure you, he's a wiser sort than all that."

"Oh, leave it to me. It's no trouble. I'll take you up on that drink when I'm done out there. I see him out there, yeah, just like you said. One moment."

Talais took the gauntlets off the table and walked outside. Brace checked the watch. He watched Talais approach Ander, who stood up suddenly. He watched them talk, measured their body language, and nodded to himself. He saw Talais smile, hand him the gauntlets, and motion toward the tavern. Ander smiled back. She took his arm and they re-entered the tavern. Brace waved to the barmaid.

"Miss? The two guardsmen coming in, I'll cover whatever they're getting first." It would take the last of his coins – and he wasn't particularly rich to start with – but a good deed's a good deed, he thought.

He closed the watch. "That might be a new record." He pulled his mug in front of his face again and returned to losing himself in the drink. "If only I could charm an elf half so well."

> "I've never needed complex ritual to satisfy my evenings. A mug of hot chocolate, a good book near a decent light and the smell of the night air carrying the scent from the garden into my window - that's paradise enough for me. I find bliss in the quiet moments where I'm entirely my own."
>
> - Memoirs of Matron Galt, Temple of the Muse

Anastasia lingered near Brace unseen. He'd had his fill of the tavern and was gathering his things to go home. The sun was starting to set in the west and a dying gold flooded the tavern. His awkward plan had worked: Talais and Ander were talking up a storm. So engrossed was Ander that he forgot Brace entirely.

He sighed to himself and muttered, "That's me, Brace the Forgettable." He stood up, holding his notebooks close, and made for the door.

"I can feel the impulse curling around inside your head," Anastasia whispered to him. She followed close behind him as he stood outside near the fountain and hesitated. "You'll spin yourself some lovely verse tonight. The tension will feed you. Once you get home, lock your door and realign your feelings from today. There's a poem birthing itself in your mind's eye and by the time you get home, you'll be ready to pour it out into the world. Or onto paper, at least."

Her eyes flickered down the street to the left. "My suggestion? Go walk by the elf's place during the Nightsong. Take it all in. Let the energy into you. You're good at that. Like I said, use the tension and power of the moment and make it your own. I'm sure you'll write the best poem you can think of."

"By the grace of the Muse, I hope I'm not being a creeper," he muttered, and slowly walked down the street.

"Just know when to stop and I can let you off the hook on this one," she whispered back, and blew a kiss.

Anathea stood up and stretched. Several maps of Spiral were spread across the table before her. Gress, standing nearby with another handful of maps, blushed fiercely.

"Your city has a strange design," she told him. "I thought 'Spiral' was just a name, not a design convention."

"The original founders were military men. They created the spiral layout of the central part of the city as a tactical weapon. They put all of the most important government and administrative buildings at the center, but built the buildings so large that they couldn't be easily scaled. An enemy would have to weather the entire spiral itself to reach the center, all the while taking hits from traps and the armed forces." Gress put the maps down and focused his vision on her eyes.

"How well did it work when Thurach came?"

He shrugged. "He took his own approach, but he didn't make it all the way. His army was whittled down and he eventually retreated. Our heroes and their doings are a matter of public record here, of course."

"As you have it. But as you built onto the city, you continued to create new spirals. This is a city of spiral roads."

"Most of the city, yes, but all the way out here, we're newer buildings. Different design philosophy. More conventional."

Gress walked to a window and opened it wide. He did the same to the doors of the balcony.

"What are you doing?" Anathea asked.

"The Nightsong will start soon. Any minute."

"The Nightsong?"

"Our tradition since Thurach was banished from our walls. There's a tower at the core of the city, rising higher than the rest, where they say Anastasia herself dwells. Every night, the muses of the temple ascend it and sing the lullaby of Spiral to us all. They have magics to carry their voices across the city. Those large metal pipes you see on most buildings, with the flared openings? That's how. People stop their work and dance in the streets while thousands of shimmerflies are set loose. Visitors tend to find it quite inspiring."

She raised an eyebrow. "Visitors? Only the visitors? You people are the ones dancing, aren't you?"

Gress made for the door. The capacity for long conversation, especially with a walking impossibility that shook his core values, had been long absent in his life. "Maybe I'm just a little cynical after seeing it every night for life. I'll send up more water to you shortly."

Anathea nodded, and Gress closed the door on silent hinges. She looked back at her maps. Ever since a dragon had kidnapped her, she'd developed a keen interest in maps before she went anywhere. She studied the layout of the streets and what was located on them at every opportunity. All the best to know exactly how to escape at a moment's notice.

She was stacking the maps underneath a paperweight when she heard the first hum of the Nightsong. It was an even tone but a pretty one. Was it a voice or an instrument? She couldn't tell. She walked onto the balcony to listen better, and saw that all activity on the street below had stopped. The people were looking at each other and smiling.

The song began. A drumbeat like a racing heart, a cacophony of silky voices, musical instruments she wasn't sure she could identify, all accompanying the most perfect soprano voice she'd ever heard. The modulation was flawless.

It was easy to think the singing came from a goddess, indeed.

An army of shimmerflies were released below, from barrels, chest and jars. They were a butterfly unique to Spiral: Larger than average with dark wings, but with chemical wells all over them that created fiery colors as they flew. They flew past her, lazy on the wind, wings wrapped in fiery patterns of gold, red, orange and light blue. One of them lighted near her on the bannister of her balcony, and as she looked at it, the wings were dark. As soon as it flew again, glowing patterns of dark blue flickered all over it.

Beneath this canopy of rainbow lit shimmerflies, the people of Spiral danced together. Lovers new and old, dear friends and complete strangers, all entwined in dance made the street a ballroom as far as she could see. Some were spinning and stepping by themselves with their own imaginations as a partner.

Anathea smiled. It was the first smile she'd broken in a long, long time. It was a beautiful smile with dimples that touched her eyes easily. She was struck by the beauty of this place. The beauty of these passionate people who called this magnificent city home.

She had come to pay her respects to Buron Hale. She was finding now why he felt, so fiercely, that Spiral was a city worth defending.

Down she went, out of her room, past Gress as he went over his ledgers without a care in the world. She went out into the street and danced with the people of Spiral. She wanted to welcome them into her heart. She wanted to feel this energy and be among them as their own. They were all connected as it was by their admiration of the heroic Buron, after all (even if her experience with him was much different than their own histories described him). There had been a part of Spiral in her for decades.

Instead, she saw people frown when they looked at her. Politely or abruptly, they turned away. Anywhere she met someone's eyes, their smile faltered. She was lucky to get an insincere nod from anyone. She stopped dancing and noticed that she had a wide berth between herself and anyone else around here. They danced, brushing shoulders constantly, but she was at least two arms lengths from anyone. No one reacted to seeing her.

Tears brimmed in her eyes. The bottom fell out of her heart. How foolish she felt, thinking as a stranger she could march in and take a place among them. There was a reason elves avoided Spiral, she reminded herself. The beauty of the city was strictly for humans. She didn't want to believe it, even snorting at the idea after having known Buron Hale.

She prepared to turn back and head inside, where she would close the doors and windows and busy herself on her maps again. Never again would she assume Spiral would welcome her.

Brace watched this nearby. He saw her joy. He saw her enthusiasm. He watched her heart chip apart with every denial, then watched it finally cave in under the apathy of the people. He knew she could have her choice of men, or any dance partner really, on her own terms. He'd heard womanizers making conjecture about her at the tavern and how they planned to hide their motivations on approach. But to dance among the people as freely as if she belonged? What an insult to Spiral!

Eels made war in his stomach. His mouth was dry and he was slightly dizzy. But he couldn't let this pass. Oh, no. Not at all. He had to do something. Something. He almost felt as though his hands were tied on the matter. Obligation!

He approached her with shy footsteps, eyes wide. "Excuse me?" He said. Twice, to get her attention.

His resolve melted as her eyes met his, and he saw up close her beauty and her misery.

He held out one of his hands. "I'm sorry about the people of Spiral. I'd be honored to share the Nightsong with you."

She froze and blinked rapidly, eyes still moist. "I think they've made clear their feelings on my being here."

"But I haven't. I have words aplenty where theirs fail in number. I want to welcome you to Spiral on behalf of the artists and creators here. Before you say it, I don't give a fiery damn what anyone else here thinks of it."

Her dimples appeared again. Her eyes flickered over him. Then she blossomed into a soft smile. She put her smooth hand into his and nodded. "I would be honored to join you in your Nightsong."

"Brace. Call me Brace." She drew close and his mind numbed again. *Power through, power through! Relax! Come on!* He let out a breath and found his feet. He hooked an arm around her waist and they danced together in the generous space offered them by the other dancers.

"You're very kind, mister Brace. You have a good heart. My name is Anathea."

"A pleasure, of course. I'm so sorry for the rudeness of my people. I promise you we aren't all so suspicious."

"This is clear, being that you're dancing with me. How is it you're so warm when they're all not?"

"I'm an artist. An artist of the word."

"Are all such artists in Spiral given over to such empathy?"

"Art without empathy is math. I've never been good at math."

"You are definitely a wordsmith. I can hear it in you."

"And you're actually glassed. I've never seen it in person before."

"It connects me more powerfully to magic, and to my own specialties with it. Better than mounting it in armor does, like your constables do."

That ended conversation for the moment. They just focused on dancing. Anathea smiled brightly, finally. The often stoic elf even allowed herself a giggle.

The sun finished setting. The sky was dark and thousands of stars glimmered above the great city. The last strains of the Nightsong ended.

They parted and Brace bowed. "Thank you for dancing with me. I'm not so given over to dancing with myself."

"The honor was entirely mine, Brace. It really was." She gave him one deep nod. "If there's another Nightsong, I should hope to see you here."

"It's a nightly thing. I can swing back by." *Dammit, was that too eager? Dammit.*

"Do see to it. I'm glad to have a real friend in Spiral."

She went back inside the hotel. Brace stood in the street both aghast at his own doings and cooling down from having been so close to her.

He noticed that none of the people in the street were looking at him, either.

Deciding not to linger, he started home. "Seems I did some good." he mumbled. His bones were light as air and his skin felt extra aware. The dance with Anathea followed him home, occasionally reminding his feet with a surprise turn or glide as he went along.

"Why do you question my contempt for the Muse-myth? Doesn't it imply that she is a distracted, irresponsible, vain deity? What help has she provided us all? I had a younger brother who died when I was fifteen. No prayer was answered, no mercy given. What kind of goddess ignores her people? Don't trouble me with the goddess. Don't talk to me about her love and passion for life. If she had such a thing maybe she'd spare one now and then."

- Argument of Rondolf Quist, founder of the Mindful

Anastasia was high above Brace as he took his leave from Anathea. She was squatting on the side of a tower, wings pulled close, watching as it came to a close. "Damn, I'm good," she said. Then she looked up and saw clouds gathering.

As they rolled across the sky and darkened, she grew rigid. Her blood chilled. "No. No, no, no."

This was not her storm. It was rolling in too fast, too far. The smell of rain came quickly. Lightning flashed in the clouds.

Anastasia spread her wings as the first light raindrops fell. Her heart felt empty and her insides tingled.

With two powerful flaps, she soared straight up. She was above the cloud line in moments. There, framed against the moon, was the Lord of Ten Shadows.

He had shed the dark mists that usually surrounded him. Here he was laid true: Twelve and a half feet tall with a smooth shaven, beautiful face and a mane of ink black hair that seemed to float around his body. His skin was snow white and porcelain smooth beneath form fitting black snakeskin leather embellished with metal spikes and rivets. A three part cloak fell across his back to ankle length, parted thus for his black wings to spread wide. The front of the cloak fell in two parts down to his knees and was affixed to him with engraved silver plates at the collarbones. He stared at her with faintly glowing blue eyes, unmoved and still.

She soared up to him, leaving a dozen feet between them. "Leave here. Please. Do it for me, if I ever meant anything to you."

When he spoke, it was deep and powerful with a rumble like thunder behind each word. The voice had no human form.

"We have responsibilities coming due, Anastasia. You and the others who have made these playpen worlds for yourselves have succumbed to too much distraction. You've forgotten too quickly that our Great Enemy is still out there."

She sneered. "Is that what we've done? Really? Maybe we've just accepted reality for what it is now. That war is over! You killed Lord Magellan years ago and we haven't seen anything more of the 'Great Enemy' since. We've moved on. We made worlds for ourselves that are outside his grasp even if he is still out there somewhere. It's the best we can hope for."

"Your world was not beyond my grasp. If it isn't beyond mine, it is entirely within his."

"How would he even know how to find it? It's so far removed from the Prime Duology. It even took you years to get here, and I'm sure it's only because you know my vibrations. Let me out of this war, Philosopher. I'm done with it all. Let me have one world to call my own and let me be the goddess I was meant to be."

"Meant to be!" he snarled. He brushed a strand of hair away from her face with long, pointed fingernails. *"You began as human as they were, thousands of years ago in another world. Have you never realized that your endowments break the world more than bless it? Who are you to chart the course of their lives? Whatever your deeds, great or small, each time you whisper in an ear, you erase a moment of choice. You suspend their freedoms for your*

whims. You compromise the gift of free will."

"No. We can whisper, but they choose for themselves. They always do. We give them ideas. They can refuse and do anything else they want. We don't control their minds."

"Would we know that by looking? How often are you refused?"

She frowned. Tears brimmed in her eyes. "Listen to me. I give them hope. I give them beauty. I'm the Muse, am I not? This is my purpose! I couldn't function anymore anywhere but here. This is a world of poetry, art, music, love. And they thank me for it. They beg me to take a hand in their lives and find them partners or advise them on passion. I'm welcome here. I'm needed here."

"You inspire their dependency on you with your every act. You've weakened them. Should they ask your permissions and blessings? Why is it yours to give? It's twice the triumph of the heart when they achieve these things without you walking them through it, isn't it? They look to you to avoid looking to themselves. If a relationship fails or love falters, do they love you then? Do you even bother to listen to the voices that curse you?"

Anastasia hung her head.

"Of course not. You're a selective listener, like the rest of the Amaranthines. Every bit as selfish and every bit as distracted. Murder, rape, death, destruction, war, grief, they all still persist in your world, unabated. Is that the will of the Goddess of Passion? Down below, there is a section of the people that hate you and disbelieve in you. The Mindful? Is that a sign of a successful goddess?"

She flapped her wings and came up to his nose. "Don't condescend to me! We all let our worlds unfold naturally. Mortal made problems demand mortal made solutions. We all agreed on that, even you! No one down there is absolutely certain I exist! We know what happens when we become *fact*. I have my faithful in the temple and a world built on knowledge and love. There have to be other variables for those qualities to mean something!"

"Small comfort to the individual you steer around from outside his perception, when you're really chasing your own selfish joys."

Anastasia's gold tears floated off her cheeks. She collected them in one hand and blew them into the clouds. It began to rain throughout Spiral. "I'm not going to discuss immortal theory with you. I left you because I was sick of how consumed you've become with hunting and destroying an enemy that hasn't been evident in long years now. He's been little trouble to evade otherwise. Is it possible he's dropped out of your war too? Perhaps Lord Magellan was the final blow and even he's finished. You never consider that?"

Philosopher lowered his eyes a moment.

"Who's selfish now? Without your great crusade, you have no more clue what to do with yourself than the rest of us do. You'd do well to have a 'playpen world' of your own. This one is mine and neither I nor it will participate in your crusade anymore. Grate all you want about whether or not I'm being selfish. I don't care. I reject your notion of obligations. Let me have this world and this peace and I'll never trouble the universe again."

He parted the clouds with a pass of his hand. The city of Spiral glittered below as a tangle of torchlight and fireflies, ivory buildings flickering in a fresh coat of rainwater. As a divine being, he could see the faces of the people from even as high as this.

"We were not made perfect, Anastasia. When we were created, our human flaws survived to taint our godlike forms. That's the core of everything that's ever happened. As you age you will slowly gain more and more power. Eventually, your most trivial thought, your slightest mood shift, will create chaos on the worlds tied to you. An accidental thought could carry global consequences. In the fullness of time, an artist below slighting you in rudeness could trigger an earthquake or fire storm that obliterates a continent. We are forever separate from them. We are not their guides or their lords

and it remains our greatest crime that we ever thought we were."

She glided up behind him and rested a hand on his shoulder. The colors there flickered to a more lifelike brown, the leather shifting color and texture, but only for a moment. His skin warmed and took on a human color. He pulled his shoulder away and it all flickered back into the colors of shadow.

"Nobody knows better than I do how much these responsibilities you've taken on have weighed on you," she whispered. "But it remains that you took them on yourself. They aren't your birthright. Turn away from all of this. We had thousands of years together before recent events. We can have thousands more. It was beautiful between us once. Remember how I all but bathed in the art of a dozen worlds?"

"Distraction. More distraction. Meanwhile, the Great Enemy holds reality in the palm of his hand. Who knows how much chaos in your very world came from his whispers? The totality of sentient life, all of it we are aware of, must be free to determine their destinies without our interference. Whether that's a glance between new lovers or the fate of worlds, the only responsible action is to remove us from the equation. We must erase the very possibility of his interference."

"Beauty is not a distraction. People can laugh and sing and dance and love no matter what their fortunes. They just have to be reminded how. They need to see and experience beautiful things that quicken their hearts. They'll do the rest. It's through these means that the divine and the mortal can coexist in harmony. We learn ourselves through our passions! We shape those passions by those works of art we take into ourselves as part of our personal experience. Everything comes down to creation."

He paused, and then turned to her. Even in this shadowy form, his eyes held regret. *"I could never be more sorry for what's to come, please know that. I know what I know. The logic is sound. My responsibilities are set."*

She prepared to speak when she sensed the buildup of power within him. She willed herself backward across the clouds. A bolt of lightning flew from his hand and arced for miles, missing her by inches. He turned and sent a bolt from his other hand straight at her.

Anastasia backhanded the bolt. It flew off course over the mountains. She hurled a globe of fiery gold energy in return, tears streaming from her eyes. It exploded against him to no effect.

"Stop it!" she shouted. "Don't do this! Stop!"

A coil of lightning gathered in the clouds and circled her, building intensity by the moment. The people below stopped and watched from the ground, oblivious to the fighting gods but awash in the light show between them.

The massed lightning leapt at Anastasia. She spun in the air and deflected it with her wing, swatting it away into a dozen different bolts that flew wild. Some of the bolts fried buildings beneath her. One struck a tree and made it explode.

She countered with a golden burst of energy from her hand. It caught Philosopher in the chest and knocked him backward, but nowhere near as far as she had hoped. He caught some of the energy coursing around his chest into his hand. It glowed, turned white, and flew from his fingertips.

She flew tight patterns in the sky, dodging his crackling bolts. She angled in on him, anticipating his aim, and double kicked him – once in the chest and once in the head.

He grabbed her ankle and swung her away. She hurtled a few miles before regaining control, and found him there, waiting with a burst of force that sent her higher into the sky.

She righted herself with all of the power she had available. She strained to stop her momentum. She conjured fire all over her body, collected it in her palms and launched it toward him.

The fire stream struck him dead on. He ignored it. It didn't even singe an eyelash.

A magnificent fireball burst over Spiral. The people were out in force now, watching the crashes of light as they erupted throughout the sky.

Philosopher flapped his wings and flew at her. Before she could react, he had crossed the distance between them and seized her by the throat.

"I'm so sorry, my love. But for the good of the universe, I must break this world. I must goad him out of hiding."

He held the palm of his hand over her heart and exhaled. He then inhaled slowly and deliberately, pulling his hand away from her chest. Crackling blue energy flowed from within her and into his hand.

Anastasia clawed at his face, but his ancient blood denied the wounds before they could be made. She went limp in his hand, wings drooping.

He held her body out at arm's length and dropped her. Through the clouds she dropped, stray energy coalescing around her form. The people gasped. They pointed. The paled. They watched the goddess fall thousands of feet. At first they whispered, then they gasped, then the ones closest enough to see her wailed.

Anastasia plummeted into a large park. It was green and good and surrounded by trees sculpted to make canopies against the sun. They were wet now, shining with rain and light from hanging lanterns.

The goddess destroyed a tall tree from on high, slamming through it and rolling away from it. The lanterns snuffed out.

The citizens of Spiral came into the park slowly. The

pointed. They gaped.

Anastasia's smoldering form stirred. She propped herself up on her hands, a trickle of blue blood coming from the corner of her mouth.

"Is that the goddess?" She heard someone gasp. Someone else said, "It can't be. She isn't real."

Shadows gathered above her. Philosopher appeared, arms wide, wings spread, looking out at the crowd.

The people screamed at him. They picked up any manner of debris available and hurled it at him. Philosopher vanished before anything made contact. It all clattered to the ground behind Anastasia.

The crowd lowered their eyes to Anastasia. She lifted herself painfully from the ground, scorch marks on her skin, a trickle of thin blue blood at her lips. They were silent. They were still.

Anastasia winced and turned away. She drew a circle in the dirt with one free hand and slammed her hand into it. High walls of gray stone shot up all around her, cutting her off from the crowd.

After a few moments, she heard their distress. Shouts. Cries. Threats against Philosopher, begging for Anastasia. She felt the mood of the crowd shift. In some people, the tragedy of the moment was already forgotten. Many saw a goddess that they didn't believe ever existed had been there the whole time, and quietly they made the equations in their mind of all the things wrong with the world. All the things that she clearly hadn't used her power to fix.

Resentment took root Only in a select few in the crowd, but they would talk. They would persuade. They would act. They were the Mindful. While they had never believed in her before, they certainly weren't going to let her obvious weakness go now. They would speak of the unworthiness of their goddess and muse and many would listen.

Anastasia wept, gold tinted tears dripping against the ground.

You foul bastard, Anastasia thought through a veil of pain. *They can see me. You made them see me!*

> **"The sun set when you closed the door.**
> **All of your light left with you, and**
> **The warmth where I drew strength**
> **Was known to me no more,**
> **betrayed by fading memory**
> **and arms that ache without you -**
> **Sailing my heart to the farthest shore."**
>
> **- Without You," Poem by Wells Kurlow**
> **(Locked in the art vaults of Spiral)**

Brace knew he had his flaws, and one was a feline curiosity. He reminded himself of this even as he veered off course from going home to make his way to the park. It was a good ways off from his destination, but he knew he had to see what was going on.

He had seen the light show in the clouds. He'd heard the explosions high above. He had seen lightning leap out of the sky and strike Spiral's highest towers.

His first thought had been to run back to Anathea, but he assured himself that she was out of harm's way. She was probably better off not being front and center for whatever the disturbance was. Besides, he didn't know yet if it was dangerous per se, and he was already closer to that then to her room at the inn.

So went his litany of excuses as he closed in on his destination. He passed intricately detailed pastel murals coating the walls of the buildings and the towering, gilded arches that framed the streets. Normally he'd give the murals a good look. Even though he was a native to Spiral and seen them over the course of his life, they were like seeing old friends.

None of this stopped him from feeding himself excuses as he wove his way through an increasingly dense crowd.

Brace turned a corner and (standing up on his toes) saw the park had changed.. Large stone walls now surrounded the park, stretching twenty feet high and somehow already overgrown with years worth of ivy. None of this had been there when he passed by this afternoon. Thousands of people were gathered around, shoulder to shoulder, talking in quick, hushed voices about the spectacle concealed within the new structure.

"It's the Muse herself. She's here. She looks hurt!" This was the general sentiment.

Brace, slightly shorter than average, found himself increasingly disadvantaged as he tried to navigate the crowd. Like everyone else, he wanted to go in deeper to see as much as he could. Like everyone else in the crowd, he was at a standstill instead.

Newcomers already pressed in at his back. He was going nowhere fast. He tried to move toward the rearmost parts of the crowd, where they seemed to be only loosely packed together. He moved through clouds of perfume and sweat with every step. Everyone was here to see the spectacle now, even the well-to-do.

He heard the city guards calling for order and to clear the way. He heard Ander's voice over the crowd. Of course he'd be called in quickly for something like this. Not that this was something common in the streets of Spiral. The city had rarely known civil disruption of any kind. Brace suspected that lack of experience would soon show poorly for the Spiral Guard.

Brace saw a spreading wave in the ocean of the crowd. They were pushing aside and pressing into themselves to let someone through. He heard, "Make way for the King of Spiral! Make way!" Brace saw only the blades of their halberds above the heads of the crowd as the King approached the Muse's new home. Brace hopped up and down, trying to piece the scene together with the quick glances he stole over the tops of people's heads.

He grit his teeth. "I never get to see the good stuff."

Brace watched the guards smash through the wall with a combined magical attack. They had held their hands together, closed their eyes, and incanted an ancient formula. Light sparked between their hands and built up to a near blinding glow. On the King's signal, they directed it toward the wall. The whipping streams of force flayed the stone apart to create a small archway.

The King motioned again, and the guards piled through. He went in last. Two guards remained behind and stood shoulder to shoulder, blocking the entrance.

Anastasia stared right at them as they entered, arms crossed. Eyes stern. She had picked herself up and regained some composure while they were chipping away at her privacy. This 50 something King with his finely groomed white hair and gorgeous robes approached her with what must have been an alien sense of confusion for him, but approach her he did. His armored men with their halberds continued to form a circle around him.

The King stared at her wide eyed, taking in her stature and processing it slowly. She was as beautiful as the stories said, but something alien as well. He swallowed hard, eyes fixed on her inhuman eyes, and spoke with a courage of a mouse challenging a lion.

"Is this true?" the King asked. "Are you really Anastasia, or an illusion? Some predator, perhaps?"

Anastasia pointed to the guard closest to her. "Zailan Cord. You are a womanizer who trivializes love. You consider women to be disposable conquests. You are seeing three women as we speak and none of them know of the others. You obsess over the beautiful and subvert it out of spite and power. You're an abomination to me. I curse you with a weak bladder for one year. Expect to go to the bathroom every half hour. Might make it easier for the women of Spiral to avoid you if you're too busy to exploit them."

Zailan's knees shook. He dropped his halberd, clutched at himself, and ran away.

She pointed to the next guard and softened. "You. Wilhela Sokar. The man you love is worthy but not as adventurous as you deserve. He's too much a safe place but he can give you security. There's another man in your life who is quiet but passionate enough that I can feel his glow a block away, and he has such eyes for you. He may be more erratic and moody, but you'd never hurt for excitement in his company. You know the two I mean. Your life may not be as secure but it would be a story worth telling."

Wilhela, shaking in her armor, asked, "Which do I go for? I don't know."

"No true goddess would compromise your free will. I won't tell you who to choose. You decide that. I'll tell you that you are worth so much to them, and being timid is approaching the point where it's a liability to you. They both sense your indecision. Investigate and choose. All I ask is that you be confident. Your fortunes are better than you thought."

Wilhela smiled broadly. The Muse waved her on, and the guardswoman darted out of the park with a squeal. The King raised his hand and started to protest, but stopped cold when Anastasia arched an eyebrow at him.

She pointed at the next guard. "You. I like your poetry but your stick figure drawings need help. I mean, really, stick figure epics? Actually, you know, the more I think about that, the more I actually kind of like it. Stick with the stick figures. See where that takes you. Surprise us both." He departed with a wave from the Muse as well.

Now, she pointed straight at King Ronmacharte's nose. "I

challenge you to doubt that I am Anastasia the Muse again."

He gulped and took a step backward. He tried to speak through a dry mouth and mostly stammered. "My...my lady, we here, I, well, the city warmly welcomes -"

He stopped short again when Anastasia walked up to him and leaned down to look into his eyes, her nose nearly touching his. "Let me be brief," she said. "I'm not here where the world can see me by choice. This breaks a law of my people. Do you understand? This is a violation of the natural order here. You and yours were never meant to see or know me to be anything but myth and legend. My one concern right now is damage control. Your job is to do anything I tell you to do for the good of the city. I don't know what I'd need you for but if I command, you obey."

"There is no other way we -"

"Blah, blah, blah. Listen to me. I feel very weak right now. I think he stole some power from me. Perhaps a lot of power. I feel depleted in a way I've never known, so I need a support network here. You are the political arm of that. Oh, I feel that little viper wiggling in your skull. Forget it. I'm not something you can manipulate and control. Also, no, I won't grant power to anyone in your family out of hand. And no, I like a nude romp as much as anyone but I'm keeping clothed, thank you much. I think I'm already in enough trouble as it is without melting your brain with cheap lusts and very damned frankly, I'm far from the mood."

She stood back up and walked away from him with a sigh. "Oh, but wouldn't that be everything right now?"

The King stood in silence for a moment. Judging himself immediately outmatched by anything that could tear down a known goddess (however fictional many might have thought her to be), he decided to shut up and listen.

"You're still here?" She asked. "I'll send for you when I need you. Go read a math book or something."

The King bowed and walked out on shaking legs.

Anastasia's legs felt no different, and for a moment she felt sympathy for King Ronmacharte V. Long had she been the most emotional of the Amaranthines. It was considered her special gift, because it kept her the most human. She laughed the most easily, cried the most easily, had what seemed to be fits of pique for no good reason (to them) and her depressions were almost unmatched. Her mood swung here and there and always to an extreme.

This allowed her to connect with the human experience more cleanly than any other Amaranthine could. Their power and perception eventually set them so far apart from humanity that they forgot so much about it. Anastasia was always there to remind them of a sunset, a baby's smile, a field of flowers, the scent of rain, anything that kept them from drifting so far into a truly alien mindset that they would lose all connection to the worlds they wanted to save.

Philosopher's words turned around in her mind, time and again. She knew he was baiting her reaction. She was exerting a level of self-discipline already that would be considered foreign to her, especially in the minds of her fellow immortals. "Anastasia in *moderation?*" they would gape. While they would do it lovingly, she knew she'd feel stung at the idea that they'd feel she couldn't be strong for herself when the time came.

She cast her power out to search for them. Amaranthines with a personal connection to each other could speak together even through different realities, as though they were standing next to one another. It might take some focus to maintain the conversation but it could be done. But no one was answering. She longed for the wisdom of Sera'loq, the sly wit of Zodiac, the quiet pleasures of Theuth or even abrasive Persephone's mechanical sense of will.

Not one answer, not one. Her lips quivered. Was she so

diminished now that she couldn't breach the walls of reality to connect with them? That must be it. Yes, naturally.

She could still read minds but not at a glance now. She had to concentrate and sift the information she needed. This should could do quickly and easily. She could only sense a couple of miles around her now instead of the entire landscape, and she had to be picky about the minds she looked for if she was straining to find a thought or feeling among them. She couldn't feel the Sleepers, but fortunately, the one she adored most was still obvious to her. Probably because she looked in on him so much it reinforced their connection.

How badly she wanted to throw herself onto a cushion in her den realm and bawl. Unflattering to her observers, she knew, but it's not like she was the goddess of hiding emotion. Her great love of thousands of years had finally finished his transformation into a monster. Was she wrong to have left him? What else could she have made an error of?

She paced back and forth, back and forth, willing the opening the King had made in the wall to be dark and impassable. Even that took more effort than she was used to.

More and more she reproached herself. More and more she felt doubt eat her confidence with cold, metal teeth. She felt like a fool. She felt so wrong. She felt so lost. She felt so alone.

Being that a stoic demeanor wasn't her custom, it was easily broken. She let the tears come. Her heart finished the process of shattering and she was on her hands and knees, letting her tears rain on the grass of the park on a wind of sobs.

She spoke to herself within her sobs. "I only ever wanted to be myself. I never hurt anyone. I tried to do so much good. Why am I wrong? Why is that bad?"

Loosely, she suspected that Philosopher was trying to militarize her somehow. Perhaps he meant to provoke anger and violence from her. What poor fortune he must have that the only surviving Amaranthines were not soldiers by nature.

Composure, she thought. *Don't let him win. Don't let him break you. You're more than this. Just find the answer. Find out. Find out who you really are. Find an answer that stands up to his infernal 'logic' and 'rationality.'*

She stood up again and wiped her eyes. *I feel so alone. I feel so horribly alone.*

It seemed almost ridiculous at first, but the goddess needed counsel. She wanted sympathy and reassurance, like she knew most humans often did in their dark times. Having been cut off from her most beloved companions, there was only one resource at hand that might suffice.

She needed mortal friends here. She needed them to accept her. Maybe if she could talk this through and feel less remote, maybe she could be stronger again. She needed to express herself. Her genuine self.

There was one person in Spiral who seemed quite ideal to relate to, in fact.

Anastasia found she could not shift or displace as easily as before now, as well. So be it. She knew she could because she felt a slight variation when she tried. So, more concentration.

She closed her eyes and centered her vision on her target. Then she breathed the word. "Come."

"Formulaic Magic is our cornerstone. It was through research and experimentation and formulae that we perfect the White Pulse, the magic that slew the dragons in the Dragon War. Creative magic, which is fueled by such uncertain things as dance, music, incantations of poetry, and the process known as creative visualization, is far too erratic and unpredictable. Worse yet, it's in the hands of too many of the common people. Therefore, we restrict the learning and practice of Formulaic Magic to government use. The sheer power of creative magic must be subverted and controlled so the people don't incite chaos against our sense of order. We must police creativity itself in Spiral so that dissidents do not unseat us with their home-grown parlor tricks."

- King Ronmacharte II to his Council

Anathea blinked.

In that moment just before that flutter of her eyelids, she was in her room at the Inn. The next, she standing before the Muse in the sheltered park. She paled and backpedaled as a familiar terror seized her.

"I'm sorry. I know you had an interesting meeting with a dragon once and you've had issues with this sort of thing ever since. Entirely understandable, by the way. Do you know who I am?"

The elf stared at her with wide eyes for a few minutes, lips trembling. There was no question about who this was. The elves had stories of Anastasia to tell as well. With the wards she surrounded herself with ever since her first abduction, it would probably be the work of a goddess to sidestep them and transport her here.

While it wasn't a dragon, it was still every bit the shock in scale.

Anathea righted herself and then planted her feet firm. She clasped her hands in front of her. "You are Anastasia the Muse," she said in a shaking voice.

"I am, and I don't want you to be afraid of me. I'm no dragon. Though Gweldon was quite friendly to you, I'll remind you. I was wondering if you would help me."

Anathea took a moment to look at the walls in the park. She heard the people outside milling about, occasionally shouting through the opening to get the Muse's attention. She smelled earth, leaves, moisture, and rose petals.

"I don't know how I could possibly help a goddess," she answered.

"You didn't know how you could possibly help a dragon, either." The goddess smiled as casually as she could. "Let me tell you why I brought you here."

Anathea nodded. She couldn't think of a long list of responses.

"You realize your name is an elven version of mine, don't you? Quor'in dialect, if I'm not mistaken. Your mother saw your full head of black curly hair when you were born and it reminded her of stories she'd heard of me. That's an odd comfort to me, if you'll forgive my vanity."

Anathea nodded again.

Anastasia shifted her weight from foot to foot. "It's becoming less an open secret and more the news of the nation that I'm real. This isn't going to go well. I'm a strange thing in a familiar world. They were never meant to see me or interact with me. My job was to be the secret blush of inspiration that prompted great art or great love. That requires me to remain aloof and ambiguous. For several reasons, really, not just that."

"You would never want the people to know you were truly real?"

She shrugged. "Enough people know me and understand me on their good faith that I've never wanted for attention here. It was enough to be acknowledged. 'Look at what the Muse has wrought! Is it not beautiful?' Sometimes they really meant me. Sometimes they meant the me inside them that they conjured up by themselves. I don't need power and worship. I just want my works to be known and occasionally for someone to say, 'this is a good thing.'"

This didn't fully click with Anathea, so she nodded yet again.

Anastasia crossed her arms. "I can't go forward until I can make you understand. When something of my power becomes a certainty, people forgo responsibility. They surrender accountability. In an all too common worst case scenario, they become zealots. Zealots aren't friends to anyone. If I remain offstage, so to speak, no one can confirm what kind of things move me in particular. There's no law passed saying that only living one kind of way matters, to sate the great Anastasia. I want people to live and create as freely as they can."

"You want art to be by everyone, and for everyone. You don't want it crafted just to suit you. Am I right?"

The Muse snapped her fingers. "Bam. Absolutely right. Faith in me can inspire the process but being a fact corrupts it. You know what's happening around Spiral right now? Almost all of the artists who were crafting epics of painting, writing or performance are redirecting their energies away from their mortal muses and toward me. They're all making art to appease me, by name. This fast, already!" She shook her head. "It's the first step toward zealotry. Meanwhile, those that didn't believe but know me now are boiling in resentment."

Anathea stood quietly, eyes downcast, as Anastasia briefly forgot herself. She turned back to face the elf and chewed her lip.

"Sorry. It's been a long a day already. And I've only been here not the better part of an hour."

"How can someone like me help you with any of that? I'm just an elf and I'm here alone."

Anastasia floated over to her and knelt down to be closer to eye level. She rested a hand on Anathea's shoulder. "You're alone here. So am I. You are exalted and hated here for your beauty and exotic nature. So am I, really. I'm cut off from the rest of my kind and my creations, so I'm feeling crushingly lonely right now. I need people. I need love. All of us do. Sometimes I just need someone to hear. I've seen your heart well enough to know that I can trust you. After all, you may be the only person in this city not picking one extreme or the other. It hasn't even crossed your mind."

Anathea marveled at the feel of the Goddess' hand on her shoulder. It was silken smooth, glancing like the softest breeze, but she could feel power in her fingers. She could feel warmth and frightening age at the same time.

"You just want me to…provide company? Really?" She didn't move but she eyed Anastasia's hand carefully. Best to let the goddess guide the dance, so to speak.

"I spend every moment of my time reveling, Anathea, or close enough to it. I'm always among them, walking past them unseen. Sometimes I take a human form and perform, too. Singing, dancing, sculpting, painting, drawing, writing. There are so many works here under pseudonyms that are actually mine. I craft them to inspire my people to create great works of their own. It's a full time job to be sure, but I love every second."

Anathea stiffened. The Muse's smile faltered.

"All of this power, all of this attention, and you let so much chaos into your world."

Anastasia frowned and stood up quickly, walking away. "Now you sound like him. That's not a compliment," she snapped.

"But it's true, isn't it? Were you watching when Gweldon stole me away? Did you see Nolek attack us? Did you stand by when Buron sacrificed his life to save me?"

Anastasia looked over her shoulder with a demure eye. "Of course, I was in the room with you. It was such an exciting story. I never saw it coming, all of that. How could I not watch? Reality has so few surprises for a goddess."

"You could have stopped it all. Buron didn't have to die, and you could have helped Gweldon, at least! What if he'd blown a gout of fire and killed us all? Would you let us die like that, powerless and helpless?"

The Muse kept her back turned.

"You would have!" Anathea's voice was loud now. Her hands were fist. "You didn't care!"

"I cared! And I'll warn you not to assume I didn't!" When she spun, her eyes were fierce. "There are *laws* among my people, do you understand that? There are *agreements*. In place since before this world was born about how to manage our responsibilities! None of us would cross those laws willingly. We know the consequences!"

"So, nothing? You would have done nothing?"

"I provide moments of inspiration, Anathea. I don't run your lives for you. Your entire world is yours to decide. All I do is try to put some beauty in it. Creating is life's ultimate meaning."

"Small consolation to Buron."

"Do you think me unfair for standing aside? Think of everything I just told you. If my kind confirms its existence we create the very kind of fierce zealotry we hate. We *must* remain parted from you all. Did you hear what I said about all those artists out there directing everything they create at me now instead of the things that matter most in their own lives?"

"How vain are you that you think people drawing pictures for you is all that matters?" Anathea shouted. "What about all the darkness in this world? Have you no care in your heart for that? They say this is *your world*. Does that mean this is the darkness in you, then? How can it not be if you just stand aside when the worst things happen?"

Anastasia's eyes mourned. She held Anathea's furious gaze for a few moments, then turned away. "So, that's how it's going to be now. First Philosopher tears me down, now the people of my own world. I was created and directed to be a Muse. It was the entire thrust of my existence, Anathea. This is the most sacred and critical part of who I am. I can't lay it aside. I wasn't crafted to be a warrior or diplomat. I was the Goddess of Passion. I am only doing what's deepest in my nature to do."

"Does being any kind of muse absolve you of any responsibility in the real world?"

Anastasia rubbed her eyes. Anathea thought, for a moment, she might have seen a tear. "I saw them disown you during the Nightstong. I thought that meant you would know what I was feeling. Did it ever occur to any of you that there are politics even among gods? Maybe, just maybe, it actually isn't as simple as you think? Has that ever flickered across your minds?"

The Muse turned away for a moment and cleared her eyes. She looked over her other shoulder. "I wish I could tell you everything. I wish I could make you understand. There are good reasons for these things. I have a specific, precise role to play in a very big picture. I am a Muse. That's my purpose. I'm sorry my world is flawed. If it's any consolation, all of them are. I've been to many. They're all the same and so many have Amaranthines in them. It's all the same."

"Amaranthines? I don't understand."

"My people. I just said that I'm not the only divine being in the universe. There are several. Once, we were united in purpose and given truly divine inspiration to guide our worlds to their ultimate potential. But we failed. We died. We scattered. We hid. Once, an entire circle of Amaranthines would have formed a council to guide this world and you would know them as gods of various concerns. War, justice, healing, and so on. Now…there's just me for this one. Believe me, believe me when I tell you, getting me was very, very lucky for you all."

Anathea held her breath and let it go. "Perhaps I'm being too quick to judge. I accept that I may have been. But you must understand my concerns."

"I suppose I should have seen it coming, true. Perhaps whatever he did to me to weaken me has dulled me a bit in my headspace, too. There's a terrifying thought." She turned to face Anathea fully. "Please. I ask you to stay and keep me company. I need at least one person here to understand me and listen to me without worshipping me or selectively hearing what I have to say. Clearly, you're the kind of counsel that doesn't mind challenging the mind of a goddess. You've already counseled a dragon! Please, stay with me a while and let me just talk with you."

The elf hesitated and nodded. "I suppose I can try. Forgive me my temper, please. I am trying to be a healer over anything else." Anathea paused. "You said 'he' did this to you. What is he? Why did he do this? Some evil god?"

Anathea's laugh was the broken glass of heartbreak. "You know what the funny part is? There's a vast war going on through many realities that's wiped out my kind. It's the sum of all of our hubris laid violently bare. It's responsible for so much I've just told you about. The punchline is, the dark, shadowy, scary bastard that did this to me? Believe it or not, he's the *good* guy."

> **"The dark of death, it beckons me.**
> **It takes my light from the world anon,**
> **Candles I have lit with a passing brush**
> **Will keep my fire forever on."**
> **- The Artist's Last Rites**
> **(Recited at funerals for beloved creators)**

Philosopher hovered above the crowd rioting in the park. His wings were spread wide but he remained invisible and unknown, save for a strange chill that passed over the people when he was above them.

He balanced a large glowing sphere in his fingertips. It radiated blue light and white bands of light shifted inside it. It was bright enough to bathe the entire city block in its azure glow, if only he allowed them to see it. This was Anastasia's stolen power, held safely away from her.

She may never forgive me, he thought. *But we are at a crossroads now. If the issue cannot be embraced, it must be enforced.*

He never liked thinking of the universe in terms of expiration dates, but he could feel a shift in the fabric of reality even the other Amaranthines would not mark. Being the oldest and most powerful of them all, even he barely felt it, but he understood the implication: The Great Enemy had stirred. It was the merest shake, but it could have all the consequences of a hundred Hells if it was what he expected. A Hell for every playpen world that wasted time for the other Amaranthines.

He looked at the gorgeous ivory spires of the city, the metal brace works the gliphids used to get about the city, the glittering sidewalks beneath the horde of people pressing in upon Anastasia's makeshift enclave. Everything about the city of Spiral was crafted to be some kind of art. There were engravings on every wall and cherubs over every arch. Fountains were built to run water on the outside of buildings, directed and redirected to be everything from weeping eyes of eternally suffering lovers to simulated rainfalls behind framed paintings.

Such a waste of purpose. Everything is a distraction. How feeble these people are. They dismiss purpose and direction to cover everything in Spiral with squiggles and sculpts. What could they have done if they directed their purposes to practical ends?

He lifted high above the city and held the sphere between his two hands, looking deep into the light. If he attuned his senses right, he could feel Anastasia's boundless love. There was no questioning the passions of the Muse. She was the most human of all the Amaranthines. She alone remembered being human and what it meant. She drowned herself in humanity, never leaving their side and involving herself in even their smallest affairs. How was it she cared so much that a pretty girl's flicker of the eye might inspire an admirer to write? What magic did poetry have without the power to shape worlds? How could watching two lovers court each other in that magnificent early days tension accomplish anything for the good of the cosmic whole?

Philosopher extended an arm and the blue sphere traveled over and under it, back and forth, until he held his fingers upward and it perched on top of them. Whispering, they called it. The only acceptable way an Amaranthine could move a mortal mind. They presented an idea, a feeling, a choice, anything, but did so unseen. The mortal would never realize that they'd heard it, but would choose to act upon the impulse or ignore it by instinct. In this way, Amaranthines had been the devil or angel on people's shoulders since...things changed. Which was not recent.

The truth was, Anastasia was probably the most practiced

whisperer of them all. She barely let an hour go by without whispering into someone's ear, somewhere. He knew she had even broken an Amaranthine law: She stopped an earthquake from destroying most of Spiral many years ago. The most anyone noticed was a shift in their windchimes so slight that they never even touched.

Yes, Anastasia was a frequent infractor of their old laws. Naturally, no one deigned fit to call her out on it. All because they loved her so. All because Anastasia alone could remind them of the most important qualities of being an Amaranthine: Empathy, love, investment, humanity. In a sense, he knew, she was the most powerful and influential Amaranthine there was, well beyond himself, in fact. Something he also knew she never took the time to appreciate.

He let the sphere float away for a moment. Anastasia had brought out his own deeply banished humanity before, and her loving caresses maintained it for years. This form was naturally colder than his more human one, but her touch was electricity to his skin. He could feel the path her fingertips would draw on his flesh as the human woke, pushing up again through the pleasures of her passing hands until he burned anew as a feeling thing once again.

Awakening the human side of him, however, would be a detriment now. He understood this. It was why he had sacrificed his human side, twice. First in becoming this thing through a Sleeping mortal life, and again when he realized this war required his ruthlessness to be won. He could not bring himself to commit the cold and terrible acts he might have to commit to balance the scales for the final confrontation. That meant burying the conscience. As he knew it would, it meant losing Anastasia when she'd fled to her playpen world instead of helping him.

He gathered the shadows around himself. This was how he was best known. A vast area of pitch black shadow with only his cruel blue eyes visible to the world. Perhaps the faintest, faintest outline of his form in the blackness would be visible if he was feeling less than attentive. Anastasia was so fearless about being herself she often went entirely nude for years on end, going before the other Amaranthines without the smallest hint of modesty. Meanwhile, he was a walking shroud of nothing, cloaked in inscrutability melded with intimidation.

Opposites attract, Anastasia used to purr.

He knew he should feel something. Any number of things. He should question attacking Anastasia and forcing her into this situation. He should mourn for what this might do to a millennia long love, one that had stopped him from being a darker thing still.

These ideas lacked the human fuel to burn in his mind. They barely registered as concerns against the icy spiderweb of purpose that directed him now, connecting him to all the different stages of his plans to see a final end to the Great Enemy. This was what he had regretted in the last moments of his human side just before he returned to being this shadowy thing. Since then, he'd felt only the crushing imperative to succeed. There were debts coming due and he intended to collect.

He would have to trouble the many playpen worlds of the last Amaranthines to wake them up to their true purpose if need be. Damn their pleasures and daydreams. The reality of the situation called to them *now*.

He looked down and saw tents being built around the park. Perfect. Her supplicants were already so desperate to stay by her side that they were going to shelter right up against the park. He saw the Spiral Guard trying to move people along and restore order to no avail. The believers would not be parted from their goddess.

Philosopher blinked. He made tempers flare below. Shouting first, then accusation, then insult. In moments, it would be fighting. It would spread through the crowd, one to another, until the entire gathering was flying fists and grappling attackers.

This anger would be an infection. Short burning but potentially deadly. Each victim would pass at least a portion of his grievance to those around him. Naturally, they would choose their own actions. It was still within the boundaries of Amaranthine law, and is the chief executor of such, he saw little reason to consider the consequences. They would choose, and he knew many would choose poorly.

There is a greater good. That justifies everything and anything I must do to see it through. Even the laws of our people are expendable in the endgame. He watched and waited.

Brace ducked a flying bottle. He made his way toward the last place he heard Ander's voice as the crowd began to push and shove in different directions. All he heard were shouts and curses.

"Ander!" he called. "Where are you?"

He certainly didn't have the physical stature to fight anyone. In a crowd moments away from riot, all he could expect was to be completely destroyed once the fighting started in earnest. Angry crowds had a habit of not being picky about who got hurt.

After too long a time sidestepping lunging groups of people, he saw his friend in full armor talking to two other guards. Other guards were standing fast and projecting a magical shield around them, forming a wall between them. Spheres of shifting golden light surrounded the guards participating.

Brace jumped and waved to Ander. "Hey! Ander! Ander! Over here!"

The guard directly in front of him cocked his head inside the bubble field. "You know that guy?"

"No, it's a lucky guess. There are ten bajillion people here and I just know he looks like an Ander out of all of them. I need to get over to him!"

"No. This area is restricted. This gathering is being classified as a riot in progress."

"How totally helpful. Hey! Ander!"

"Please disperse back into the crowd and stop attempting to distract the guardsmen."

"If I disperse back into them it'll be like throwing glass at a wall. I'll be killed in there!"

"Step away from the barrier, please."

The guardsman's bubble popped. Unshielded, he looked at Brace through the narrow eye slits of his helmet with wide eyes. "Huh. Well. That happened."

Brace walked past him with a glare. Ander had dropped he guardsman's shield himself by tapping it with the crystal on his gauntlet. "He's with me. Shield up, please."

The shamed guard looked away and restarted his shield. He tapped both crystals on his gauntlets, made a complex two handed gesture, and the field restored.

"Sorry. New guy. What the Hell are you doing here, Brace?"

Brace rolled his eyes. "The Muse herself falls to the earth and people wonder why I'm here? I made an offering to her earlier today."

"C'mon, you're smarter than this. You know this is going turn into a storm any moment now."

"I wanted to see if they were right. I knew there'd be a crowd, but this is sort of an order of magnitude above that."

"She knows how to make an entrance, that's for sure. If that's really her."

That's when the crowd ignited. The shouting doubled in volume and went from isolated shouts to hundreds of people barking at each other – alternately cheering fistfights or yelping as they were being hit, it all joined together into one sharp, staccato noise. Objects of every type flew over the crowd. Brace saw smoke starting to arise from two locations in the crowd just inside his field of vision.

A guardsman shouted, "Press out! Subdue and disperse!" The bubbled guardsman did another hand sign and their bubble shields turned red and doubled in diameter. They marched forward slowly, stomping one foot at a time and in unison. Everyone their shields touched received a mild shock.

Anders turned to Brace and said, "Go home, Brace. There's nothing for you here right now."

"How can I go home if she's really in there? My gods, to actually just see the Muse for a second. She's supposed to be the most beautiful woman that ever lived."

"That's what everyone else is thinking. Look where it got them."

"But what if she leaves before I can see her?"

"Brace, for your own good, get the Hell out of here. I can't protect you here forever. I don't know what's going on with her or if that's even her, but it's not bringing out a good side to people right now. Just get out of here at least until the riot's put down, okay? C'mon, buddy."

Brace's heart imploded. "I could have seen the Muse. Just to see her, by everything right in the world."

Then reality shifted. He was inside the park walls. He saw Anathea standing there looking bewildered. Then he saw the Muse herself, calmly standing in the center of the room.

Here he was, humble Brace, bracketed by the two most beautiful people in all of creation.

He looked at them both, wide eyed, tongue tied, sweating. Then, he fell face first into the dirt.

Anathea raised an eyebrow. "Did he just faint?"

Anastasia shrugged. "Beats vomiting on your shoes."

"They call it practical thinking, but they make me feel like everything I love is wrong."

- Princess Petrenella Ronmacharte

Anathea rubbed her eyes and scowled. "Suddenly, this all seems so familiar."

"What's wrong? I thought you liked this guy. He was very kind to you. I thought maybe some friendly company might comfort you." Anastasia cocked her head as Brace stirred in the patch of grass he'd landed on. "Sorry about that, though. I'm not used to anyone doing, you know, that. When I summon them. That's new."

"The summoning!" Anathea said, shaking her head. She rolled her eyes and walked over to Brace. She knelt down and tapped two of her chest crystals. She waved a hand over his head and said, "Somehow, you intoxicated him bringing him here."

"I'm sure he'll be fine. It'll clear up in just a bit."

"That's not the point. We're three people who are essentially strangers to each other trapped in a closed space with something bad happening outside. Remind me, where have I done this before?"

Anastasia chewed on her lip. Then her eyebrows perked up. Brightly, she said, "No dragons this time! There's that!"

"But there is some monolithic shadowy superbeing-thing of your type menacing us from on high. The rest of us are collateral damage in the making. At least the dragons I met were somewhat reasonable."

The Muse sighed levity evaporating. "I promise you, I'm bending all my thought on it, whatever it looks like. I know he doesn't want to kill me or anyone here outright. Believe me, with his power, he could wipe out an entire continent with a wave of his hand. He's the only Amaranthine powerful enough to kill others of our kind. This is one of his damned, condescending object lessons, I'm sure of it. Not that it doesn't make things less potentially dangerous for anyone."

"All of this is an object lesson?"

"Let's say the two of you are of one mind about my failures in the universe." Anathea winced from the sour tone in the Muse's voice now. She hadn't taken into account that a voice as emotional as hers might shape injury into a such a casual but wounding rebuke.

"Judging by the riot, he's not really concerned about safety for the rest of us."

"Believe me. He isn't."

Brace's eyes fluttered. "I can fart 'Hello' in three languages."

Anastasia waved him off. "Well, one, but he's not entirely wrong."

Anathea rolled her eyes. "Fascinating."

"So, listen. I have a plan. Everyone around the park saw me fall and they know I conjured those walls. Some of them have caught glimpses of me in here. You can see by the riot how this is going to go. I need to get out of this enclave and retire somewhere to figure out what to do next. I think Brace here is a good place to start."

Brace smiled, his eyes closed, and said, "I love bean dip."

Anathea's eyebrow rose. "Are you absolutely sure about that?"

"Of course. Bean dip is precious." Anastasia tried a smile.

Anathea shook her head and stood up, unfazed by the Muse's return to humor.

An old man in gilded gold and purple robes marched through the doorway. His robes had golden arcane sigils drawn all over it and he wielded a tall wooden staff, hand carved with arcane incantations and gems of every color encrusting the shaft. He wore a golden metal skull cap fit to his head with an amber colored gem set above his forehead.

The Muse threw her hands up. "Oh, by the Travellers' grace, not *this* guy. How did you get in?"

"I am Cappus the Wise," he bellowed. "I am the head sorcerer of Spiral and -"

"Shut up, already. Spare me."

Cappus looked at her with his mouth agape. "W-what?"

"I don't need to hear some long, pretension-heavy title about whatever deeds you're proud of. Spare me the opera."

His mouth opened and closed a few times. Then he cleared his throat and pointed his staff at her. "You have denied the King of Spiral. I am here to out you as a fake!"

"He tried to do that already. Ask him how it went."

"I am more wily to the arcane ways of demons and intruders than the good King. I am here to save Spiral from the chaos your nefarious plot has unleashed!"

Anastasia smiled broadly and clasped her hands. "Are you now? That's delightful! Tell me, did you stand in front of a mirror and rehearse all of this before you came today? You really hit that whole threatening staff pose with such conviction!"

Anathea looked back and forth between them and knelt down beside Brace, putting a hand on his back and muttering a protection spell.

"Enough of your falsehood, demoness. For the sake of Spiral, I banish you!"

The wizard slammed his staff into the ground. The walls shook and a blinding light erupted from his staff.

Anastasia made a pinching motion with her fingers and the light extinguished with a loud *PUUH.* A trail of smoke coiled upward from the polished wood.

Cappus brought his staff to eye level and stared into the darkened gem on the top, which now had a magnificent crack in it.

He spun on one foot, swinging his staff in circles, building up a potent magical current that left glowing trails of motion from the simmering gems. He then swung the staff wide with a triumphant cry, sent a wave of searing white energy toward the Muse.

She held up one finger. The wave parted and hit the trees and walls behind her. The trees shattered, the wall burned, but Anastasia was untouched.

As the trees fell behind her, Anastasia slowly blinked her eyes. Just once.

Cappus straightened his robe. His face tightened with determination. He waved his hands about and summoned a spark of fire that ballooned into a raging fireball. He slung it at Anastasia, who stopped it in mid air by holding up one hand. She flicked her fingers and it turned into a giant snowball. She let it fall and break on the ground, and simply let it melt.

The Wizard studied all of this for a moment and nodded. Very casually, he said, "I admit, you're pretty convincing."

Brace suddenly sat upright and scooted away from something in front of him. "Chickens! No, not chickens!"

Anathea cupped his head in her hands and pushed him back down as the two forces in the room stared at each other.

"You're going to tell the King and the people outside that I am, in fact, fake. I was a cruel illusion cast by a trickster demon who wants to subvert the people's will. You will tell them that you banished me completely and that I was a lowly denizen of some other world rather than the goddess who stands before you. Then you will press charges on the instigators of this riot and return control of this place to the King. You will tell them that you are doing what you can to track the demon and punish it for this vicious prank."

The Muse's voice was even and direct. Cappus paused for a moment to take it all in and nodded.

"One more thing, since I have you here, Cappus. There are two kinds of magic in Spiral and you've heavily restricted one while indulging in the other. Shall I describe how you've done so?"

"M-my Lady, I-I don't...."

"You have focused on the fading art of Formulaic Magic, scientific arcana, to the exclusion of all else. Incantation, arcane equations, tried and true methods, traditional learning, all of these things. You've ensured that this magical potential is reserved for those rare few in Spiral with the money and time for the rigorous educational systems you've set up to teach them, only to graduate them into direct service of the King. You keep major magical powers for yourself and away from the people. For security and safety, of course.

"Meanwhile, you hobble all of my artists in this city with laws to restrict the viewing and sale of unlicensed art. No one is legally allowed to express artistic ability unless directly authorized by the Creativity Commission, as you call it. They can show it to family or friends but they can never display it on the streets. You call it quality control. You want to ensure that the city of Spiral is known for the greatest artistic achievements far and wide in this world, but you do this at the cost of silencing generations of talent for what amounts to your own vanity."

Anastasia slowly walked toward him, her wings twitching with every footstep. Cappus backed away. "The truth is, you know the magical power inherent to true creative potential. You know it to be a second magic as potent as any of your dusty rationality. Your system was created to *restrict* the best artwork made in this city so that the magic possible through the soul and the mind can be kept silenced. That way, no one can compete with your government's advantage in ruling the people. There are vaults under the palace chock full with the greatest art made over the last generation in Spiral. Books, plays, music, paintings, sculptures, everything. You only let the mediocre go forth into the streets."

She motioned with her hand, and Cappus lifted off the ground to Anastasia's eye level. She leaned in so her nose almost touched his. Softly, she asked, "Now that you know who I am, how do I feel about that, wise one?"

"After Thurach, we realized magic needed to be controlled! Too many loose cannons, too many variables we couldn't contain. We couldn't let magic go unregulated in a city this size! There was no way to predict who could wield creative magic or to what extent!"

"I know. Cappus, creativity is also a quality of human potential. The soul can't grow without expression. Smothering Creative Magic is only making it stronger. There are private practitioners of Creative Magic everywhere in Spiral. They know to hide it and they keep it as a quiet thing to themselves, but most are using it to do good. Imagination spun magic, that's the next big thing in this world. Formulaic Magic is dying for a reason. Even in my diminished state you couldn't touch a hair on my head. I also know you've never seen or banished a lesser anything in your life, and you were practically wetting your robes before you came in here."

She lowered her hand and he fell into a heap, helping himself back up quickly with his staff and backing away. "I'm going to address those silly restrictions soon. After today I can see the need for things to change. I was allowing your oppression only because it allowed the underground art community in Spiral to thrive brilliantly. As of now, I no longer care for the powers of reason ruling over my people with such an iron hand. Go, run along and do what I've commanded. Remember that stories of my temper are not kind things to hear."

Cappus scurried away without another word.

Brace shouted after him, "Remember my pants!"

Anathea pushed him back down again. "That's at least more like the goddess I've heard about."

"Half measures. Too many people have seen me. If I were at full power I could wipe their minds with a flick of the wrist but not this time. I've already tried."

What she didn't tell Anathea was that the battle against the wizard was more taxing than she had let on. She did her best to look untroubled through the process (a Muse has her pride to consider). In the end, though, deflecting those spells took more conscious effort than she'd ever exerted in anything before. As a full Amaranthine, she could have wiped him out of existence and erased all trace or memory that he ever existed in the world with so little as a yawn. This was a level of exertion she was not prepared for.

She snapped back into the moment when Anathea asked, "Doesn't that fly in the face of the free will thing we talked about?

"I think you'll find being a divine being is far more painful and complicated than you imagine," the Muse hissed. "Do me the temporary kindness of not judging me for every little thing I do."

Anathea pressed her lips shut.

"So much damage has been done and will be done. Cappus' decree might mitigate things, but probably not. It'll just slow things down for a few hours at best. The one thing I know Philosopher will do is fan the flames. The only comfort I have is that we're not dead."

"What is his object lesson supposed to be? You don't have any idea what all of this is about?"

"I think so. He wants to show me how my presence among you all poisons your souls no matter what I do." She jerked a thumb toward the outside world. "He's making a great point of it by barely doing anything at all."

"They say the Muse has taken many human forms. They say she has made love as both a man and a woman. They say she's been old, dark skinned women and young, eager eyed blondes. They say she's talked with barmaids in taverns and kindled their passion for painting, modeling and art. They say she's counseled poets and sculptors while posing as family members. She could be here now, one of you listening to this, smirking at her own cunning. I'd love to share a laugh with her about that one day."

- Saylin Oronda, most popular actress in Spiral

Brace smelled the familiar aroma of his room. The scent of habitually burnt incense, wood and old books. He swam in the place between awake and asleep, distantly aware that his body was lying down and at rest.

Then he smelt an odd smell, like rosewater. It was pleasant, really. His mind tried to unlock the connection. Rosewater, rosewater.

The elf.

Then his mind screamed silently, The elf is in his room!

He pitched himself out of bed and stood straight up, still clutching his bedsheets. Anathea was sitting on a chair beside him. The glow in her left hand gem winked out.

"Uh, hi." His fingers clutched the bed sheets the way a warrior clutched the straps of a shield.

She pursed her lips. "I have to admit, that was pretty impressive. From sleep to standing up in less than a second."

"What are you doing here exactly? I mean, it's not that you aren't welcome, just...what? What happened?"

"We've come here to lay low. I'd normally be at the Inn but

considering how people are behaving with the riots, I didn't want to be easy to find. I remember the Nightsong."

Dread crested in his heart. Yup, this was his place. Polished wooden floor that hadn't been swept in too long, bookshelves lining the walls with books thrown around inside them rather than properly set, a dish by his writing table with a half eaten donut.

He gave her a sidelong glance. "When you say 'we,' you mean...?"

"Myself and the goddess."

His jaw gaped. "What? *What?* You brought a goddess *here?* Are you slippin' serious? And how did you even know where I lived?"

"Well, you told her she could come here, and she figured it out from there. You know, 'goddess' and all that."

"I told her she could come here? When?"

"You were unconscious but she spoke to your mind." She looked around the room. "I understand your reservations. Your housekeeping skills are pretty lax, I have to say. I think Anastasia called it 'completely demoralizing.'"

He pulled the covers up over his head. "It's a place owned by two bachelor guys," his muffled voice protested. "It wasn't meant for goddesses! Or elves! Or anything, really!'

"Relax. It's not like we don't have bigger concerns. We haven't seen your room mate, either."

"If the civil unrest is still going he'll be staying at his assigned barracks. Security measure. Is the riot still going?"

"A few of them. People aren't doing well, being denied their goddess. It's been an interesting two days."

He peeked out, wide eyed, from beneath the blankets. "Two *days?*"

"You had dislocation sickness. It's rare but it happens to people who are summoned through space from one point to another. Your mind had to realign itself. It's like hitting a bump in the road that jars your teeth. You were largely intoxicated the first time. You cleared up slightly and discussed things with Anastasia, but the second time she did it to take us here? You didn't wake up right away. You've been recovering since."

"Two days." He examined pajamas and bed sheets. "How did I eat or go to the bathroom?"

"I'm a trained healer and responder. I took care of it."

He blushed fiercely at the idea and pulled the blankets back over his head. They ballooned outward with a humiliated sigh.

"Please don't be put off. I've trained for healing my entire life. I was looking into getting a job nursing at one of the local hospitals. I figured they'd have much use for me, given my leanings. I've seen far, far worse than anything you can show me."

"That's not the point. But where's the goddess now? What is she even doing here? Why does she want to be here?"

"She thinks if she diminishes her signature further, as she worded it, maybe this Philosopher thing won't find her easy to track. She's taken a human form for the moment and she's trying not to use any special powers. We'll see how long that lasts. Right now she's just watching the world from here. She looks like a muse from her own temple. I suppose that makes the most sense."

"And we still have riots."

"Mostly in the city area surrounding the park for a few miles. Outlying districts of the city are still skeptical but the discontent is spreading. There's a lot of anger and frustration. Having seen a goddess fall from grace, they want answers. You know how humans get when it comes to suspense."

"I'll take your word for it. Can you leave so I can get dressed?"

"Needless modesty considering what I've just told you, but certainly."

Anathea left. Brace dressed himself awkwardly, a numb feeling racing through his intestines. Loose black pants, a blue tunic, his brown leather jacket with the golden quill stashed inside a deep pocket. He buckled a belt and looked at himself in part of a broken mirror. Good to go, but he saw the worry in his own eyes and tried to hide it.

He would never deny that he was physically interested in Anathea. She was amazing and he wasn't dead. Yet, the way she clinically dismissed his body just now had stung. Oh, maybe it was a pipe dream to think someone like *that* would be so taken with an average fella like himself as to find him desirable. Somehow, though, that didn't seem like the point.

He had his dreams, that was the point. The uncertainty of knowing either way what was or wasn't possible - that had been a comfort. The tension had been delicious even if it did grate on him at times. Now, that what-if was completely ruined in the moment she passively discussed caring for him like he was an infant, moved in no way whatsoever by his masculinity or his good will. He was in the cold valley where 'maybe' became an absolute 'no.'

His room remained slightly cluttered. They'd obviously cleaned it out a bit while he was out. He wondered where all of his other clothes were, save the outfit they had left for him – a tunic, pants, undergarments and boots. Nothing fancy. Then again, he doubted he owned anything fancy.

Anathea was in the hall as he came out, putting the last of the house's hourglasses in the closet.

"What are you doing with those?"

Anathea shrugged. "She says hourglasses are bad portents.

Reminds her of an 'Amaranthine she'd like to forget.' I asked her about it and she just shuddered and changed the subject."

Brace shrugged back and walked left into the kitchen, keeping an eye on Anathea as she stacked a few more boxes back up in the closet. She had to rearrange some of the storage space for the hourglasses. The wood paneled kitchen was in no better a state than his room, but she said nothing about it now.

There goes that golden moment we danced. All wasted. I didn't even have a choice. What could I have done? It's not my fault. This is so unfair. He picked up a cookie from a wooden plate nearby. Chocolate chip, and fresh! He picked up a few more just to be on the safe side.

"Where is the goddess now?"

She struggled to get the door shut, then threw her body into it to get it to latch. "Do you want to talk to her?"

He was going to answer, "well, obviously," but stopped . He had no idea what to say to her. What kind of conversation do you have with something like that? Do you talk about the weather? Nice job creating snails? Isn't it nice how the sky is on fire during a cloudy sunset – was that your doing? Bravo for clouds!

He finished off the first cookie as Anathea double checked the closet door. He was aware he hadn't answered yet. She probably didn't expect him to.

"She'd probably like to talk to you," she said. She gave the door a satisfied pat. Enemy vanquished. "Perhaps a little more than she did when you were absent minded. I've talked to her much over the last two days. She's...told me so many things."

"She's a goddess. Can't she just pull the conversation out of our heads?"

"She's says she's much diminished right now, remember, and she's trying to keep her powers low key even beyond that. Don't make assumptions. I don't know what passes for low key among her kind, powered up or otherwise, but it wouldn't do to be rude to a divine being."

He coughed into his sleeve. "Well, okay, that's true. Where is she?"

"She's been standing on the roof watching the city. I think she's watching the riots. Again, I don't know how closely She's taken a human form so she's much more like us at the moment. You'll find her. There's an absence of people standing on your roof."

Brace scaled up a ladder onto the roof of his house. It was a modest house in a modest neighborhood nearer the Outer Reaches of Spiral, so not the fanciest of all things. It was a two bedroom house with a living room, a kitchen and a small den, probably better suited for temporary students for the university down the street than two bachelors making an honest go of it. The roof was flat but firm. He and Ander had put a small table and a couple of chairs up there to look out over the city over stiff drinks on some nights.

The humanized Anastasia stood near the edge, looking out over the houses at the pale spires of the city and the smoke rising from the streets. Brace stopped dead in his tracks.

He stared open mouthed at the frozen music of her form. She was pale skinned now, with a cascade of long brown hair that fell well past her shoulders and stirred in the soft breeze of the rooftop. She had expressive blue eyes that danced with charm and as he looked her, she smiled a smile that lit up her face. He understood now how inexpressive most faces could be just beholding how vibrant her features were. Her pouty lips could shape any mood perfectly, and the corners of her eyes held an unfettered joy at seeing him. If Anathea had stripped him of words to describe her beauty, Anastasia stripped away his ability to reason, to do anything but stare in wonder at the face before him. Words and wit utterly deserted him.

His eyes drew down over her now. The rest of her was no less remarkable. She was much exposed, and he remembered that Anastasia was definitely not the goddess of modesty. She wore a small, chain maille bikini top, and a thin metal strap on each hip held a sheet of knee-length white fabric in the front and back to preserve what modesty she had left. No sculptor in Spiral could have caught her dimensions and do them justice. She was formed as only a goddess could be, a living statue who made every breath she drew a work of art. She was human height now, equal to him, but every inch an impossible goddess.

Inwardly, he was able to question how anyone could see her like this and *not* assume she was beyond human. As disguises went to conceal divinity, this one failed completely. He could think of no other sane reaction than to look away. He felt a fierce blush burn his face.

"Hello, Brace. I felt you stirring downstairs." Her voice was a lullabye. He imagined it could stop a charging beast and he imagined it could purr like a kitten. Every word was flawless in its articulation and clear to his ears. She spoke with confidence.

He swallowed hard, looking up and keeping his eyes focused on hers. "I've never met a goddess before. I'm not sure exactly what to say." If his mind was blanking on conversational points before, he certainly wasn't going to conjure them up now.

"You'll find we're surprisingly approachable as long as people are honest about who they are. Self-deception is understandable but it is irritating after a while. Thank you for letting me hide out here in your home."

"Well, as a goddess, couldn't you make any home you want? Or make someone take you in?"

She pressed her lips together and shook her head. In a voice even and controlled, she relayed to him the events between her fall from the Heavens and the current moment.

"All of this is because some shadowy bastard wants to teach you a lesson?" Brace sat down at the table but kept his eyes on hers.

"I think so. I'm assuming. Again, like I told Anathea, it's my only working theory."

"No offense, but I'm glad I'm not in your shoes. If you wear any."

"Usually not, but I get the idea."

"What do you plan to do now? Just watch? Wait?"

"I need time for people to disassociate from having seen me. Let skepticism and denial take their place. That wasn't going to happen if I stayed smack dab in the park in my natural form. The riots are already going full tilt as it is without me walking around in plain sight."

"Well, let me be fair. That's not the most, ah, incognito disguise."

"It's the garb of a temple muse at the Temple of, well, me downtown. Nothing could be more fitting."

"I dunno, I thought maybe you might turn yourself into a dwarf, or a gliphid, or a turtle or something. That's as incognito as it gets. You're sort of...standing out, you know? Looking like...that on a rooftop in this neighborhood."

"Not to worry. Nobody's noticed me yet. Maybe I'm just starting to get my energy back a little. I've been resting and practicing for two days and I can hide myself from mortals again, I think. At least for certain periods of time. I'm picking up my mind reading but it takes an effort now and it's not as informative as when I was full strength." Her eyes scanned the skies. "Getting my unseen nature back even in part is his doing, I'm sure. He'll want me to walk the city and see the fruits of my labors."

"Will you?"

"I think so. I have to know what's going on. The reports are that nineteen people are dead from the riots and over fifty injured." She withered then, her eyes wide and downcast, the corners of her lips pulling down as she hung her head. "All because they saw me."

His heart went out to her. Was it as simple as seeing a pretty girl cry, or because this was unexpectedly vulnerable for a divine being? He chalked it up to a combination of both, chided himself for one and internally nodded at the other, and leaned forward on the table. "How do we reverse this? There's surely something we can do."

"You need to focus on Anathea right now. Let me deal with my immortal problems."

Brace blushed. Of course, Anastasia would know of his tension for Anathea. His heart inflated suddenly, though - work on Anathea? Did this mean he had *the Muse's* blessings to pursue the woman? Was his situation with her not lost after all?

He leaned in on her, any reservations about talking to a goddess rent asunder. "How do I work on her? To what end?"

"She's lonely and confused. She came to Spiral for a reason. You've been a good friend to her. She could use the counsel of someone like you."

His heart sank back down again. Oh. Anastasia was referring to a different connection entirely. He folded his arms over his chest and tried not to look as disappointed as he felt. He also knew Anastasia would probably see through that in a heartbeat, anyway.

Brace moved the conversation forward in hopes of distracting her. "You're kidding. Me? She's an elf and one of the most gorgeous creatures in all of creation."

"Pardon me, gorgeous *women* in all of creation, if you don't mind. And what am I? Chopped liver?" She spun on one foot and winked.

"You are unsurpassed, I promise you. No one's ever going to argue that." He let his eyes wander over minute details of the roof instead of looking at her. "But you're the most unattainable woman I can imagine. I'm already dealing with the second most unattainable."

"Brace." When she approached him, he whipped his head up to look her in the eye, trying to tune out the rest of her form for his own sanity. "Before you get too far along, I'm going to warn you. I don't promise mortals to one another. I don't give my blessings to you people and I don't just randomly assign you to one another no matter how much one party begs me to. I whisper, I nudge, but I stand back and let nature take its course otherwise. You understand that, right? I can't help you win her over in any way without betraying one of the most important things I believe in."

"Which is what, for the record? What does a goddess believe about these things?"

"Great is the freedom to love who you choose, Brace. I've seen incredibly unlikely pairings in my eons and they've been some of the happiest relationships you could imagine. Believe me, there were struggles to overcome and even hearts broken in the process but I know what I'm talking about. If she isn't attracted to you, I'm sorry, but haven't you won the treasure of her trust? Is that worthless to you?"

Brace turned away and walked to the edge of the roof. He kicked a can off the ledge and listened to it clatter below. "I don't know how I can stay sane wanting her as much as I'm starting to and being confined to myself in spite of it."

Anastasia cocked her head and her tone changed. "So, that's it, already. I'm surprised at you, Brace. You're too selfish about her. That's what the problem is. Let me guess, you've written a script in your head about how she's going to be, what she'll be like, the things she'll say and do, all of it being things that make you particularly happy and feel at peace. Of course. I wonder, if I reach into your head and look, will I see her being submissive and playful and endlessly smiling?"

"Please don't look in my head. I'm humbly requesting you don't do that."

"If I wrote a list of things that would not incriminate you, that wouldn't exactly make the cut."

"I can't help it, okay?" He spun on her, eyes pleading. "I'm not a wizard of love. I'm a human and I'm flawed and I only have what's going on in my headspace to think of. I'm not evil, I don't kill people, I don't steal from old women, nothing like that. Please don't judge me."

"'Please don't judge me' is likewise not the best thing to say to an immortal. Apparently that's exactly what I'm supposed to be doing." Anastasia walked toward another ledge. "I'm going to walk the city and talk to my people. I can't decide what to do next, but I've come more and more to the thought that I need to interact with them for a change to see what I'm needed to be. Meanwhile, I have something I want you to think about."

She mounted the ledge and turned to face him, soft hair stirring in the breeze. "All you're thinking about right now is how to twist and turn things to make her a big part of your life. Have you stopped to consider even the first thing about hers? How much time is she going to have to grow into herself if you smother her? Don't become your own worst enemy here, Brace. I can't tell you where things between you will go, but you're way too smart to be defeated by your own covetous eyes."

The Muse stepped backward and plunged off the roof. Brace ran to the ledge and looked down.

She was gone.

He leaned back and wished he had a strong beer. He looked up at the clouds rolling through the Spiral night. "All I did was walk by the Inn," he muttered. "That's all I did. All I did was just walk down her street. I can't even believe all of this."

"It's a burden to be told to smile constantly. I don't care about making you happy as a complete stranger if I'm busy being wrapped up in my own problems. I don't owe a smile to anyone just because."

- Kaitlyn Norah, Spiral dramatist,

from "Where Tragic Blooms the Flower"

It was away from expectation that the Muse's mood could bloom. The social pressures of being a goddess were surprisingly painful. She tried to remain calm and stoic before Brace and Anathea, and upbeat, if anything.

The truth of the matter was, she was anything but cheerful. She chewed the inside of her cheeks and walked with her shoulders slumped forward, hugging herself as she went. Her head was hung and her eyes tight with grief. She consciously willed that no one would see her, but barely paid enough attention to her surroundings to see if it actually worked.

It was long known among the Amaranthines that giving direct evidence of their existence was detrimental to human minds. For one thing, being confronted with puppet masters (and as much as she hated it, that was the proper word) who were both immortal and incalculably godlike often drove them into madness. Deference became worship all too quickly, and the smallest praise or reward would be blown out of proportion to be something far beyond the intent. Human minds either became absurdly zealous or profoundly bitter. Given time, each mortal mind would edge toward one or the other. Their egos, their sense of self-determination, were always a casualty.

Normally, the gilded arches over the streets were filled once a day with incense. Usually a different aroma for each day of the week.

The placement of the incense, within burners hanging from the arches, allowed the scent to float down the streets for most of a day. Not overpowering, but a sweet touch to the air. Today was supposed to be rose petals, that would have been replaced with mesquite coming the Nightsong.

But not today. Instead, she could smell the smoke and blood, even blocks away. This was her beloved Spiral now. Where once her people danced and sang with the Nightsong, now they burned buildings and lunged at each other. Believers attacked nonbelievers and vice versa. Shopkeepers fought looters with whatever they had on hand. Buried grudges saw opportunity to resolve themselves, accountability lost in the shouting crowds. Statues of her were being torn down all over the city.

Yet, for what? Why? She was the one beaten down by a dark and shadowy force. Because she lost the fight? Because she was proven to exist beyond doubt? The implications of such things often drove people to hysterics, yes, Philosopher was right about that. The mobs in the streets were proof of that. They had just seen what had amounted to their lord and savior cast down and brought low, only to avoid them completely. Such an event had consequences..

There wasn't much point in hiding and whispering now. Yet, she dared not go before them en masse and claim her godhood.

Walls seemed to press in on her from every direction. She felt short of breath at times. While she wheedled on whatever to do next, caught in her sense of defeat and indecision, her city was burning and the people dying. *But how to keep making things worse?* She turned it over and over again in her head and found no plan.

All of this, *all of this,* from merely glimpsing her when she fell. All of this because they encountered a passing moment of her vulnerability with their own mortal eyes!

Two days ago, she was dancing with joy among her people,

delighting in all of her favorite things. Now, she skulked in those same streets in human form, desperate not to be seen. To be brought low so fast and so easily!

In a long ago time in a far away world, in a civilization buried by time itself, she had been a slave as a mortal. She was purchased from a slave master for a very high price, being beautiful and proportioned like a goddess already, even in her original living form. She was all of sixteen summers old and absolutely terrified. The man who bought her had dark eyes and a darker appetite, and made clear that her degradations would be many and foul. She was a toy, nothing more, and she had little hope of meeting a kind end if his vicious appetites soured on her.

Away she was taken, wearing a chain and nothing else, led through the busy marketplace with a pull on her collar now and then to remind her where to go. She averted her eyes, studying the rough hemp of the rope that bound her wrists. Her feet were sore from walking along the dirt streets, pulled as she was over any manner of obstacle without a moment to catch herself. She kept her breath still as she could. Easy feat, since her lungs barely functioned as she considered what was to come. If only they could stop breathing that very moment.

It was as bad as she knew it would be in his manse. He slaked his appetites on her without a hint of mercy and made a profit from his friends doing the same. Every inch she lost of herself, she became something else. She drifted further and further away until she said nothing, did nothing, felt nothing, and was dead to all the world in her heart of hearts. This catatonia brought laughs from her abusers but otherwise went unregarded. They weren't there for conversation…

But her dreams! She had such vivid, powerful, colorful dreams. Dreams of absolute freedom. Dreams of running through damp grass after a sunrise, running towards the sun in pure joy, smelling roses in the wind and heart light from her cares. She felt the sun on her skin and laughed. She would plunge into the waters of a large pond and backstroke until she could float. She'd stare at the clouds above and smile. She was in a vast, round place where the walls were decorated with the finest art and gorgeous, spiraling columns formed breezeways within. She had designed it herself with her inner eye.

Over time, this became all she knew. She had forgotten the weakened flesh she was used for. But over time, this other her began to realize the crimes done to her, and slowly a fire blossomed in her heart. Slowly, she realized she wanted freedom in both worlds. She wanted peace. She wanted to find this dream place and run in the sun for real.

More and more she became lucid again, and became calculating. She saw that she was written off as mentally derelict, and that careless means surrounded her now. Her shackles were looser. Food was left half-gone on nearby plates that she could eat, left by her customers. She sampled nearly drained wine. She stared around the chamber she was held in and lost herself in the paintings.

All of this sensation, under her own terms, began to empower her. There was a world outside these walls filled with such treasures, and better yet, the people who created them. She wanted to talk to them. She wanted to dance with them and let the smile in her eyes touch their eyes. She wanted to laugh with them over wine, and above all, she would beg them for the secrets of their craft. How could they do such things? Conjure pictures out of plaster? Find sculptures in clay? Find the stories in blank parchment? Hear the music they could make for others? It enthralled her until it became her true passion. Locked in that room she had ebbed like a tide, and was now rising to herself in truth.

Her master had come to her one night full of wine. She had hidden away a knife someone had left with their food. Assumed to be catatonic by all now, no one suspected the trap she'd laid. He taunted her and she laid still, staring at the wall with her lips slightly parted, giving no reaction as usual. He laid close against her to take his pleasures.

She put the knife straight into his neck. His hand cupped the wound. She stabbed again and again, embracing the feral moment. He went down easily. His look of wide-eyed horror would be a sadistic pleasure for centuries.

She slicked her wrists with his blood and pulled her shackles free, loose as they had been. Customers had complained about bruises on her flawless skin. They wanted her unmarred. What was the point of tightly shackling an invalid?

She stumbled away from her cushions. She went to the painting on the wall she loved most, of a coliseum where great entertainments were held, and hugged it in her outstretched arms. She peppered it with kisses and promised herself she would find the artist. Her inner world was based largely on this design.

Thus was the promise, at least, before her master's two friends charged into the room and stood fast long enough to take in what she had done. Her life flashed before her eyes, two lives in one – the dreaming life and the broken life. She was weak and her sneak attack was spent. She knew they would turn on her and she would be beaten to death or strangled in mere seconds.

They moved upon her. Something grabbed the face of the nearest one and slammed it backward into the wall so hard he burst open like a melon. This savior figure grabbed the other man as he spun around and threw him into the opposing wall with enough force for the same result.

There he was, then, before her. He was the most perfect man she had ever seen, with long flowing golden hair and blue eyes, such strange blue eyes. It looked like he had extra pupils in the colored parts. He wore layered white leather armor with all manner of engravings, with gold rivets holding it all in place. He had a purple cloak that fell in three sections against his back, but she didn't know why. Gold plates with the faces of the gods emblazoned upon them buckled this cloak and its two long front portions to his armor at the collar bones.

"I've seen enough," he said, and his very voice warmed the room. She felt the cold vanish from her. "I couldn't let this happen to you. You're a dreamer and you have a powerful soul. I was meant to find your kind and prevent them from coming to this."

"You're not going to kill me?" she'd asked, strangely numb to it if he could try.

"Kill you?" He smiled a sad but gentle smile. "I'll make you immortal. I'll give you the power I have in some quantity. You'll grow stronger with time and you'll share my purpose. I'll keep you safe from all nightmares. But you have to trust me."

"Me? Immortal? Powerful? Why?"

"Because for you it's a good fit. I can see into people's hearts. I would know better than anyone. You can do more than enjoy all this art you dream of. You can inspire it, for hundreds, if not thousands of years. People will shower the world in poetry because you asked them to. They'll write stories, sonnets and song. The sculptor, the actor, the drummer, the painter, they will worship you. You will be first among the court of muses. I will give you everything you ever dreamed of."

He held out his hand. She looked at the bodies in the room and a chill passed her. "Is this part of it?"

"Not for you. Not ever for you if I can help it. I'd prefer you took another course."

There was, in truth, nowhere to go. Nowhere to hide. No job to be taken, and as a slave who rebelled against her master, death was assured. She had fantasized that she could be clever enough to escape detection, but knew in the real world she would be dead in a matter of hours, most likely.

So, she reached out. She took the hand of her benefactor. She was taken away into another world where she was Changed.

She became the youngest of the Amaranthines, but the most passionate and playful. Now her heart exploded with love and feeling. She cherished her extended family of immortals, but immersed herself in humanity and the arts. She created a den realm identical to that of her dreams, and her first act was to run through the damp grass in the rose scented wind and hurl herself into the cool waters of the lake, propelling herself along with her golden wings as she searched the skies above.

In time, she ruled a court of Muses, capital M. The Amaranthines had created her and her court to remind them of the humanity that all too often fled them over long centuries. Their touch was to nurture the wounds of the ages and remind them of the passions of life. Without this they would emotionally sicken and become something like Philosopher was now. She had a powerful purpose.

She'd always known that his approaching her openly and saving her had broken the laws of subtlety of their kind, already considered before she was ever known. He had gone before her in a diminished version of his true form, but he had gone before her still. Because he had come to her in honesty, she believed in him. She felt the warmth and the meaning of it and reacted to it on an all too human level.

Thus, she began to doubt whether hiding was actually her best course of action after all. She had conducted herself until now in the way she was commanded to by the Amaranthines, being unseen and acting through impulsive whispers. Now the certainty of her prevailed in her world. She wondered if it might be a bad thing to actually embrace it instead of running from it. Was there a way she could step forward and not poison the world? Would Philosopher expect that?

There was only one way to know. She would visit some of her favorite personalities around Spiral as herself. She would talk to them privately and gauge their reactions. If they became zealous and overwhelming, well, add that to the swell in the streets. But if she could get them to believe her good intentions and respond to them...

She quickened her pace. Anastasia knew exactly who to talk to first.

The blind sculptor named Pyrek the Old.

> "You can save someone against any enemy except themselves. That one wins almost every time."
>
> - Andili Tamos, Mindful advocate and mental researcher

How do I fix things now?

This was the question that ruled Brace's mind. There had to be an answer. Somewhere in the vast reach of the universe, there was an answer about how to recover Anathea's interest. Surely it was possible. Hadn't they shared something special? Didn't they bond? Wasn't it obvious how great they could be with each other? If only he could open her to that.

He hadn't money to buy her gifts. He hadn't status to woo her. But they had the Nightsong! If only it would play again. He'd extend his hand just so, and lure her back into his arms for another spin around the sidewalk or two. Surely then she'd let go of any pretenses. Rather than be the woman who tended his inert body for two days and all the humiliations that came with that, she could be someone who shared a divine spark with him. She seemed so controlled, so stoic.

So far, anything Brace did to melt the ice with the elf had failed. He had tried small talk by asking her why she had come to Spiral in the first place, and found that this not only failed but prompted her to scowl and close off even tighter than before. He tried cooking for her, but needed her assistance to put out the fire. (How he managed that trying to fix her a bowl of cereal he would never know).

He tried drawing a picture, but the stick figure offerings that amused his friends brought no levity here. Defeated, he tucked his golden quill into a deep pocket in his jacket.

Finally, after his attempts to engage her in conversation about recent events, she stood up from the rather worn couch in the living room and said, "I'd best be on my way. I have my own room elsewhere. I have valuables there that I'd like not to lose and I could use the decompression time."

Brace's heart sank bank into his stomach. As casually as he could manage he said, "Well, I should walk you home, at least. That would be courteous enough considering there are riots all over town."

"I have defensive magics that will serve me well enough if called upon to protect myself. I'm in no danger."

Pursue, or back off? Brace didn't know. But he had scant heartbeats to decide and every half second he delayed made whatever answer he gave more awkward. He knew only that the worst thing he could imagine right now was being parted from her.

"It's a gentlemanly thing to do, all the same. I'd feel better to know you got home properly."

"That puts you at significant risk. There's no point endangering yourself when I'm perfectly able to get home safely. There's no reason for it." She wasn't trying to be evasive or cruel, he realized. She sincerely didn't see the point of the gesture.

Brace accepted his defeat and let his eyes sink to the floor. Anathea finally read the situation and rolled her eyes while he was looking elsewhere. "Very well, Brace. Perhaps I could do with a guide who knows the streets better than I do."

He jumped up immediately. "You won't regret it, I promise."

She regretted it.

It wasn't as though Brace did not have his charm. He was quite capable of it, although that might surprise him. Anathea could read his attraction easily enough, and that had not immediately put her off.

It was how jittery he became when he felt his interests were threatened that started to shift things. This gallant artist who had danced with her in the Nightsong amidst those standoffish citizens now seemed to be falling all over himself trying to make impressions of a much more shallow nature.

This gesture to walk her home, for example. Brace didn't have the magics or experience that Anathea did. To be fair, it seemed like the young writer was fond of his mug and his meat above any martial concerns. If rioters did attack, she'd spend more time trying to protect them both than anything else.

Yet, she saw that his concern was genuine. In this case, it was coming from a good part of his heart. He genuinely wanted to be there if something went wrong and she knew he would do all in his power to protect her from harm, however ill advised his attendance. Perhaps it was better to humor him like this than to have him sulk on his couch, feeling broken hearted and dejected, while the city plunged into violence around him.

She still doubted it was a wise choice, and walked the streets with Brace gritting her teeth, making sparse conversation, wondering just what the right answer in this situation would be.

"The Hanging Library isn't far," he told her. He pulled her into a doorway while a couple of young rioters ran by with burning torches. Fire and smoke clouded the street but it was otherwise empty. "We can probably get there through a couple alleys I know of. I shortcut through them all the time."

"You want to go through back alleys in the middle of a riot?" Anathea didn't want to tell him that the nasty smell he commented on somewhat earlier was burnt flesh. No need to worry him out of hand when he was already this jumpy.

"Keeps our visibility low and ensures we don't have to watch all sides, at least while we're going through the alley. We just need to be quick."

"What do we want from a Hanging Library, exactly? Shouldn't we keep on the move?

"The Hanging Library is suspended fifty feet off the ground. It was made by hollowing out curved Wensfellow trees. It's shaped like a ring, too. We can get in and travel a couple of blocks out of sight and off the ground. Take ten minutes off going be the streets."

She arched an eyebrow while she looked up and down the street. Well, Brace had his uses in this strife after all.

They agreed it was clear and ran down the alley beside them. Brace took them down two more.

Anathea saw it then. It was a structure that ringed a park for half a mile, supported by huge metal supports sculpted to look like angels lifting it off the ground. It curved around the exterior of the reading park, where benches and tables with now-torn awnings dotted the grass. It looked like a series of giant logs that someone had carved windows into. She guessed the inside must be at least forty or fifty feet across as well.

Brace took her by the hand and trotted up the golden staircase leading up to the doors. Anathea gently pulled her hand free but followed anyway.

He came to the locked doors and knocked. They were hand-carved to resemble two closed books pressed together, pages first.

A gliphid's purple nose inched into view in the two thin windows flanking the doorway. "Go away! We'll have no rioters here! We didn't order any!" Anathea heard the gliphid suppressing his extra vocal cords to have just one voice. The extra voices just grumbled behind his words.

"We're not rioters! We're trying to stay away from them!"

"What a riotous thing to say!"

"Look, we have no torches or weapons, we just want to cut through to get to safety!"

"Sorry, the doors are locked for the duration of the crisis. It's the city's edict! We don't dare defy the laws of the city!"

Anathea stepped forward and said loudly, "I'm an elf of Salvaron and I'd like to stay alive!"

The doors unlocked and swung open. The small gliphid took halting steps forward, running a hand through the tuft of blonde hair capping his head and wearing a green preserver's smock. His black bead eyes were wide. "An elf. Whooooooa. You're the elf everyone's talking about!"

"Yes. I'd also like to not be lit on fire, or worse."

The gliphid beamed, grabbed her hand, and hopped up and down. "Come in! Come in! Come in! Look, everyone! I found an elf!"

Brace closed and locked the doors behind him. Rows of polished wood bookshelves curved around lush red and gold carpeting, creating a circular area for the large round reading table in the center. Behind this were more rows of books on more conventional bookshelves. There was a vanilla smell from the candle sconces in the walls.

More gliphids appeared, jumping onto the table, the chairs, and hanging from bookshelves. Easily a dozen. Each was a different hue of purple and they stared at Anathea with ink black eyes. They oohed and ahhed over her, each in the same type of smock.

Her usher backflipped onto a chair and smiled at her. "I'm Nibs. Nice to meet you! I'm one of the Bookitechts here. We make sure all the books stay in good condition! What do you like to read?"

"Well, I'm not here to read, I have to say. Brace and I are trying to get back to the Inn I'm staying at. Do you know Gress and his

Inn?"

"Oh, Grumpy Gress, I know that guy. Stays to himself. If you wanted quiet, you sure went to the right Inn."

"Actually, it's been anything but. My friend says here's a way through here to where we need to go."

"Oh, can't you stay? We've never met an elf before! I know, we can perform our favorite selections for you! We read a lot and we share our favorite scenes. We can perform them, like a play!"

"I'm so sorry, Nibs. If we can get through the riot in one piece, I promise to come back and visit you all. Right now I need to get back to my Inn. All of my things are there and if they still are, I went to look out for them."

"You'd come back? That's amazing! We have an elf friend!"

The gliphid backflipped again, landing perfectly on his perch while the other gliphids rejoiced. This time, thin black gems fell out of one of his pockets. Anathea levitated one up to her eyes.

"This is a memory crystal!" She looked at Nibs, aghast. "What have you people been doing here?"

"That's not a memory crystal! That's, ah, a playing piece. We gamble here. For fun. That's a chip."

She closed her hand around the crystal. "Trust me, I know what a memory crystal is. This one's inscribed with glyphs if safekeeping. What are you doing here?"

Brace stepped forward. "There have been rumors of memory theft around town. People creeping up on drunks and stealing a memory or two, then selling it underground through illicit markets. People buy emotions this way. Love's first kiss, a baby's sigh, a hug at your most vulnerable. They go for big ring coin to certain people."

"You've been trafficking emotions?" Anathea inspected the

crystal again. "Is that even legal?"

Nibs hung his head and shuffled one foot on the chair. "Well. Maybe not in the strictest sense of the word." He brightened. "But we do it to spread positive energy! This way everyone can know what it's like to fall in love at first sight or read a grand poem. Not everyone understand how to do that themselves. It helps the world!"

"You can't buy and sell empathy," scolded Brace. "This is supposed to be a city of beauty and art. You're stealing people's ability to relate to it and selling it to others best served learning how to savor these things themselves!"

"This has a recurrent seal glyph," Anathea continued. "It's reusable as long as it retains some charge. That's complex magic. Who's doing this for you?"

Nibs simply hung his head. "We thought it would help people."

"Selling it only helps you." Brace drew the gliphid's smock pocket open with his finger. "How many of these do you have in there?"

Nib slapped his hand away. "Look, you guys want to cut through, right? That's fine. Just leave us to our business. We don't mean any harm and neither do you. We don't need to be at odds."

Anathea tossed the crystal back to Nibs. "I should tell you, we're on speaking terms with the Muse. We've met her. I'm going to ask her about this when I see her next."

"You met the Muse? People outside say she died in the park."

Brace crossed his arms. "She's pretty talkative for a corpse, then. Quite an eyeful, too."

Nibs looked back and forth between them, and then his shoulders slumped.

"Maybe you know her, maybe you don't. I don't know. We're just trying to eat. That's all. We love our jobs but it doesn't pay much here. We honestly thought we could make people happier this way."

Anathea hardened. "The memories you take with these are *gone* from the owners. You're letting everyone else sample their memories like a beer in a tavern party and keeping it away from them forever. You're doing harm whether you admit it or not."

"We only take them from people who do bad things!"

"Which will serve to make them colder and even worse."

"Do they deserve to hoard what good things they keep for themselves when some weeping poet or lonely child might do better with them?"

"Who are you to judge, Bookitecht?"

Nibs quietly fumed, eyes averted.

"Brace, let's take the long way around. I have no stomach for memory thieves."

Anathea whirled on one foot and made for the doors.

Brace took a moment and looked at the room of quiet gliphids.

"I loved this library. My dad used to take me here every week for something to read. I love those memories. I wouldn't want to be near anyone who'd steal that from me."

As Anathea and Brace unlocked the doors again, Nibs ran a finger through his pocket, sorting the memories. He pulled one out and looked at it in the candlelight.

"Wait, elf. The goddess had a special one made and gave it to us. She...knew you would be coming here. I didn't know if we should give it to you, but perhaps if I do, it might calm your harsh words,"

Anathea stopped. She turned and looked at Nibs, silent.

"We don't know what's on it. But we know her. She came to us last night and told us who she was, and we believed her. We couldn't look at her and think her less than a true goddess. Who could? She asked us to make it for the visiting elf. Then she put something into it and left it with us. She said she was keeping it for you as an apology, pending how things turned out."

"Why didn't she keep it herself and give it to me?"

"She seemed to be quite busy, and I imagine she's too busy even now to address it herself." Nibs shrugged. "Also, she didn't have many pockets."

Brace touched Anathea's arm when she started to move forward. "Hang on. We have no reason to trust these little bandits."

"Anastasia came and went over the last two days when you were asleep. It's entirely possible she came here. She could have even whispered into your ear to come here when you started out again from your place. She probably knew you'd insist on coming with me. You just flew on a course she determined."

Brace scowled and lowered his hand. Anathea stepped forward and took the crystal. This one didn't have any sealing glyphs. One use and it was done. Something swirled inside it.

"I'd not use it now," suggested Nibs. "But the Muse said you'd feel so much better afterward."

"Did someone steal memories from me?" She searched her mind for anything that indicated a lost memory, but even with her intimate knowledge of memory crystals, she sensed nothing wrong.

Nibs shrugged. "If anyone did, it's the Muse. Not us. If it makes you feel better, she's did scold us about the memory thing. We've been overwriting these with complete book texts since she left. She gave them the power to absorb the text of a book and return it to a new printed page or empty book elsewhere. We're preserving again, but in a different way." He sniffled. "I'm sorry about everything."

Anathea stroked his cheek. "You really aren't bad little creatures, are you?"

"We never intended to be."

"Brace, let's cut through and be quick. We're fine for the moment."

"If you believe them!"

"I do. Thank you, Nibs. I'll only open this when the time comes."

"We were so excited to meet you!" Nibs said, smiling again. "Skarps will take you guys through. Will you ever come back?"

"Depends on this crystal. But I won't rule it out."

Nibs smiled and waved as Skarps hopped over to guide them. "It was nice to meet you, mostly! The grumpy guy, too."

Brace frowned but followed Anathea through the library.

"I began the world as empty as any other human hourglass. I am heavy with accumulated time."

- **Pyrek the Old**

"Pyrek the Old" was not some clever name. He was eighty-five years old and had seen Thurach with his own eyes.

He was fifteen years old at the time and had already made a reputation for himself as a promising sculptor. He had soft and smooth features then, and his broad shouldered frame was popular with many teenage girls.

Most of them died when Thurach came blasting through the city. Thurach had ignored the spiral design meant to tactically channel enemies through a long gauntlet of military counterattacks and made a straight line towards the center of the city, destroying everything that stood before him. His Dragon Sworn minions – reptilian things corrupted by dark dragon blood – had swarmed the city for miles, slaughtering every living thing they came across.

It was unbridled violence, savage and careless. Thurach was eventually turned back and his forces scattered. From the people rose the hero Buron Hale, who ranged far and wide to hunt down and destroy the Dragon Sworn wherever they could be found.

Before that, however, Pyrek lost his eyesight. The toxic blood of the Dragon Sworn had splashed across his face. Healers had smoothed out the scarring across his face, but his eyes were destroyed. There was no recovering them.

Pyrek spent two years in self pity, but his hands felt a familiar pull to the clay. One day, concentrating as hard as he could on the image in his mind and making his hands follow suit, he crafted a new sculpture.

Over time, he crafted more. Surreal, beautiful pieces that expressed a pure emotion from inside the darkness that took him. His work sold well, and he began to live well. Until the government of Spiral decided to license art and expression for "quality control." He invested his resources and lived comfortably off the interest, creating art now only for himself.

Anastasia had watched all of this and swelled with pride. He wasn't sure if he believed in her or not, but he loved the legend, and invoked her name reverently. As many young males did, he had gawked at the statue of the Goddess in the temple and the many things they draped her in, all seeming designed to flatter her physically, and as many young males, he had his steamy daydreams that the Muse would descend on him one night and...validate him, in many ways.

In the end, however, he thought her but a pleasant daydream, yet he talked to her in lonely moments as if she could hear him. He enjoyed the myth. He was playful about it.

She had listened to him every time.

He was sitting in the second floor room he called his home. It was small, with a bed, a desk, a dresser, and a table. He had no need for candles but had lit them for the smell. He had stood by his window, curtains drawn, listening to the discontent as it occasionally passed by.

Anastasia appeared in the center of the room. She allowed the creak of the floorboards to announce her.

"Who is that?" the old man asked.

"An old friend, really. You've invoked my name many times in your life. You've dedicated art to me out of whimsy, but still you dedicated it. I'm thankful for you."

He paused, his mouth opening and closing for a moment. He stood straight and composed himself. He wore modest robes with long sleeves, and pulled it down to adjust it. "I've heard that the Muse fell in the park. People swore they saw her. Are you Anastasia the Muse?"

Anastasia moved toward him with silent foot steps, then caressed his leathery cheek with her hand. He shuddered at the power in those finger stroke. The softness, the light, the sheer divinity. It seemed to leave a trail of pleasant fire in their wake that faded like a candle's dying warmth.

His arm trembled. Haltingly, he raised it and let his smooth old hands brush against Anastasia's human face, feeling the shape of her cheekbones, her eyes, her cheeks and chin. The sculptor's hands erased all doubt.

He shook for a moment, then got down on his knees and bowed.

"Please don't," she said. "I'm not worthy of that kind of thing. I'm convinced of that now."

"You're the Muse herself. I swore all my life you weren't real!"

"I know, I heard you. You've also spoke to me in privacy throughout your life. You've wished I could be real with all of your heart. Here I am, now, Pyrek. I'm very real, and you've always been one of my favorites."

She helped him up by one hand. "I've come to talk to you, Pyrek. I know you don't have much time."

He nodded sadly, holding her hand but unsure whether to continue doing so or to let go. "I'm on my way out, divine lady. Lung malady. I have a month and change, they say."

"I'm so sorry. You've lead such an amazing life, though, Pyrek. You're a shining example of expression. I'm very proud of what you've accomplished."

Moisture appeared against his dead eyes. "You liked my work? You felt it was, well, honorable?"

She smiled, and she let him feel the smile. "You were brilliant. I celebrate you. I have some of your sculptures in my private den realm."

He covered his face with his hands. It took him a minute to stabilize. She waited patiently.

"What wisdom can I possibly give you?" he asked. "You say you've come to talk, but it's said you could hear words without talking."

"I want to know some things and I feel you're an important touchstone. Will you talk to me?"

"Every artist begs a conversation with you, my lady."

He was so heartfelt that she couldn't help a blush. She asked him, "You were blinded but you carried on. Why?"

"Don't you know why?"

"Voice it for me. Put it in your own words. I'm not peeking into your mind."

"Because the dark cannot stop me from burning bright."

"How did you know that was true?"

"I'm not sure. I felt that if I concentrated hard enough I could shape the images I could still see in my mind. I know as the decades wore on I must have forgotten exactly what people look like, but people embraced the imperfections in my art. I pushed onward because I was alive and I would rather fail doing what I love before succeeding at doing anything I hated."

Anastasia nodded. "I've lost so much of my power recently. It was taken from me by someone I trusted. Now, he parcels it out to me. He allows me to go unseen again now because I know it suits his purposes. But I am not the power I was. I am not the goddess I was."

"I hadn't heard that you had enemies, my lady."

"I didn't know I did, either. Not this particular person. But he robbed me from myself. Compared to the others of my kind, I'm weak now. My miracle are few and uninspiring. Without that potential, can I really be the Muse?"

"And you liken this to blindness?" It wasn't a rebuke for her notion. He asked kindly.

"You were trapped in a dark place and you pulled yourself out of it almost single handedly. I'm looking for that kind of conviction now."

He nodded to himself and retreated to the table in the room, finding the chair beside it without help and sitting in it. "What do your powers account for now, then?"

"I may be as little as one tenth as powerful as I was. That covers a lot of ground, believe me."

"Still superhuman, though."

"Well, yes, in every respect. My feats still look godlike to any mortal's eyes. Some of my best tricks take a lot of focus, now."

He shook his head.

"What?" she asked. "What have I missed?"

"Have you ever spoken to me before?"

"No, never. I've watched you and listened to you but I've never spoken to you until now."

"You've not influenced me in any unseen way?"

"I could have, but no. I never did."

He leaned back. The chair creaked. He let out a long exhale.

"Anastasia. You have never exerted your power over me in my life and yet I have done what I'm told are breathtaking sculptures for decades. Decades. All the while I thought of you, whimsically, sometimes with ignoble ideas, but I have done so. You inspired me even though I barely even believed you existed, if ever. I ask you, is that not power? The mere idea of you carried me forward over a lifetime of creation. And yet, you did nothing."

She stared at him.

"These things you can still do, these other things that make you powerful: do you believe it's power that makes you divine? Do you need to crack continents and swallow storms to prove yourself? To whom? Who judges?"

She joined him at the table and sat in an opposing chair. "But the others of my kind, how can I pull my weight with them? How do I do my part? I've always been part of a divine community. Now, I'm too weak to properly call myself one of them."

"That's your sin, Anastasia. Forgive my boldness accusing a goddess of sin, but there it is. The most important thing I did as an artist was to stop comparing myself to other artists. It made me fail and it made me jealous. It made my hands inaccurate and muddied my vision. When I let go of those comparisons, I realized myself anew. I ignored critics. I ignored comparisons. That, my lady, is when my work started to soar.

"When I learned to create for myself and someone, maybe even just one person, in my intended audience, everything changed. My work stopped being about everyone else and became about something in me. The secret messages I sent to steamy crushes, beloved friends, bitter enemies in my art, it didn't matter if anyone else knew them. It mattered that I did. I let go of trying to please the crowd." He chuckled. "Being struck blind freed my creative mind. It taught me to create within myself."

Anastasia's eyes searched the floor for a moment as she processed it all.

"You're right," she finally said. "You're absolutely right."

"Say it. Make it official. I want to hear you say it."

"I don't have to compare myself to others of my kind. I never should have. I am...I am no less a goddess to my people for what he's done. I am still me."

"You forgot that, didn't you? Whatever this 'he' did to you, he didn't cripple you as much as you thought. No, his trick was *blinding* you. You couldn't see what you were anymore. That's it, isn't it? I always thought you had no power and existed as some sort of friendly spirit, unseen but begging to be entertained. That's one myth. I never calculated greater power about you. Did I do all of these things for you over the years and talk to you over my shoulder because you had power? Or because you were you? I loved everything about the idea of you. What else would I need to know?"

She stayed in silent. Was it so simple? He continued on.

"Forget the burden of judgment. Forget comparison. If you've been drained of your power, remember you never needed it to be our goddess. We all loved you beyond it."

Anastasia stood up and took his head into her hands. She kissed his forehead. "I'm sure I could have read all of that from your mind, but honestly, it wouldn't have been as true as hearing it from your lips."

"It's my honor to inspire you the way your myth inspired me for so long. What will you do now?"

"I have other places to go in Spiral. I need to talk to more people. I guess I'm rebuilding myself. Or maybe I'm teaching myself that I can rebuild."

"More importantly, give yourself permission to rebuild into the goddess you really are."

Her eyes glittered moist as she caressed his cheek. "If only I'd talked to you more often. We could have been great friends. I'm sorry for that."

"You talked to me through your inspiration. That's dialogue enough for a lifetime, isn't it?" He patted her hand. His was so old and pale.

She helped him to his feet and told him, "Name anything you want. I'll give it to you. Do you want your eyes back? Do you want eighty more years of life? I think I can do them. Maybe not as easily but I think I can do them."

"I've lived long enough to become obsolete in my own mind. I've had my time. I feel dislocated now. I'm a victim of my own antiquity. As for my eyes, leave them. This is who I became. I assume you can't restore your own power easily, so I would be greedy asking you to restore me. It would be unfair."

"What then? What do I give you?"

"Isn't it obvious, my divine lady? Kill me."

Anastasia gaped at him. "Kill you?"

"My road is ending. Nature is taking its due and not a moment too soon. I've done my part. Don't let me go out painfully. This will be a bad death, I'm told. I'm in pain enough most of the time now as it is. Please, just ease me out of this world softly. Let me exit with some dignity."

The corners of her mouth turned down. Her eyes were wide and suddenly dry. "Are you absolutely sure about this?"

"Maybe now is the time you should go back to reading minds."

Anastasia read him, and saw the truth.

She escorted him to his bed, where he loosened his robes and swung his feet up onto the mattress. She pulled the blankets close to him and tucked him in. "I'll make sure you're never forgotten. No one will forget Pyrek the Old and his amazing sculptures."

"That would suit me just fine, my lady. Thank you for coming to me. This is the great honor of my entire life. I can't tell you what it means to me to have met you."

She smiled, but only slightly. "Don't worry. I can see it. Thank you for counseling a lonely goddess."

He patted the hand on his cheek. "Be well, my Muse. Never stop dreaming."

She smiled and bent low to kiss his forehead, numbing all of his nerves and ushering him into a peaceful sleep. She willed his heart to stop and sent pleasant dreams of his youth to his mind. He died reliving the happiest moments of his life, far from pain.

"Farewell, friend." She lingered near him and said, "I wish so much I had talked to you more."

"We are hungry for despair.

We cheer it on in our loved ones.

We delight in a hero's fall.

We oppose the hopes of others.

We laugh at painful accidents.

We poison you through ourselves

And delight in failing with you.

For if our dreams can't succeed,

We'll be damned if we endure your own."

"The Cynic's Curse," unknown author

(Graffiti found on the Temple of the Muse)

Brace tackled the rioter nearest to him. It was a sloppy lunge but he hoped the rioter was as inexperienced with fighting as he was. At the very least, the bearded man in the soiled gray shirt and worn breeches didn't seem too bright, so he seemed a safe bet.

They rolled away together, and as soon as Brace got to his feet and put up his fists, but a gold blast from Anathea sent the rioter through a store front. She turned and blasted two more aside, energy leaping from her hands and cone-shaped waves.

"Run!" Brace shouted to her. "Stop that and just run!"

They'd knocked away the closest enemies. The small group of rioters had surprised them as they came around a corner and immediately attacked them, the Hanging Library not two blocks behind them now. Brace could guess why: The elf was a coveted prize, to kill or to do unto otherwise. He was ready to kill if he had to to prevent either outcome.

"Run where?" she asked. Her crystals glowed gold and she released another shockwave, sending two rioters flying backward a dozen feet. "There'll be more of them here any moment!"

"Anywhere we can lose them!" He grabbed a nearby club. He guessed it had been a table leg to a large dining table once, but now it was used merely to attack. "Anywhere but here!'

Anathea drew up next to him, defaulting to his word. Brace felt his heart lighten in spite of itself. *She actually listened to me! Maybe I can get her out of this. Maybe she'll feel better about me.*

He motioned to follow and he took off running. Anathea ran while blindly launching more shockwaves behind them. They came to a dead end, but he helped her up onto the top of the glitter-encrusted brick wall there and followed up himself. They hopped down onto a pair of trash sacks beyond it and ran toward the opening of the alley.

"No, Brace! In here! Look!" She pointed to a series of steps leading down to someone's basement door.

"What? Why there?"

"Running around is going to make sure we meet more rioters. We need to catch our breath!"

He grunted, then ran down the steps and tested the door. He saw the sign above it said SVETIK DRESSES. Anathea stood next to him, charging more offensive spells and watching the top of the stairs.

"Locked! I don't think anyone's home. Dammit."

"Pick it then!"

"That's breaking and entering!"

"This is a full scale riot, Brace! We need off the streets at least for a little while! Come on, get it open!"

He began searching the area. "I need something small, like a stick or a pin or something. I…" He grabbed at his jacket, then pulled out the quill. "Ah! This might do it."

"You're going to pick the lock with a quill?"

"Since I'm not a professional thief, I'm sort of having to improvise." He slid the quill into the lock, and instantly the door opened. "Huh. I didn't even do anything really. That's a terrible lock."

Anathea went inside first, hands glowing, and Brace followed her. He shut the door on a darkened room. The only light came from the streets, falling against a wooden table and several flagons of wine. Several limbless mannequins held up a variety of finely tailored dresses, providing mute audience to the intruders.

"Maybe we can barricade the doors with the flagons," she said, and began to pull a flagon over toward door.

She stopped, looking at Brace in the dark. He became aware of a soft golden glow in his hand.

He held up the quill. It wasn't enough to see by, but it was untouched by the dark.

"What….what is this?"

"That looks like a feather from the Muse's wing! It's about the right scale. May I see it?"

Brace handed it to her. She studied it closely and said, "I saw her wings before, when we talked in the park. I swear this is right off of her wing. It's the right size and shape and look, that glow."

He blinked several times. "I've been writing with the wingtip of the Muse herself?"

"She didn't mention this to me before. Where did you get this?"

"I bought it at the temple. I'm reasonably sure I bought at the temple, a few hours before all of this started." he rolled his eyes. "The Muse loves these sneak attack gifts, doesn't she? Your crystal, my quill…"

"Have you been writing better?"

He shrugged and put his hands in his pockets. "I guess my writer's block hasn't been so bad. And I've been consumed with wanting to write all the time. Except during a riot that's wracking Spiral, anyway."

"I wonder what else this can do." She took the tip and threw it a nearby stone wall. It buried itself in the stone like a dart.

Anathea and Brace both stared at it. "Did you know it could do that?" she asked.

"No. How did you know?"

"I didn't. I wanted to see what happened."

"You just randomly threw the Muse's feather at a stone wall with no idea what would happen? Seriously?"

"Well, what else was I going to do with it?" She pulled it out of the wall and handed it back to Brace. "You have a blessing there. But you say you bought it from the temple!"

"As far as I know, they don't sell Muse bits there. In spite of any graffiti saying otherwise."

He walked up to the stone wall and shifted his grip to hold it like a pen. He began to write, and the words appeared clearly on the stone. TESTING TESTING TESTING. They appeared in a glowing script that cooled into clear black writing.

"And she didn't mention this to you? That I had it?" He turned it over and over in his fingers as though any new angle might reveal more secrets.

"Maybe it isn't a big concern for her right now. She clearly has other things going on at the moment."

Brace sat down in a chair at the table, staring at the feather. "I'm holding a blessing of the Muse. If not for recent events I might never have known it. I might have run this quill dull and thrown it away like any other."

"That thing just cut stone. I don't think it's going to dull."

Finally, he smiled. "I'm going to write a poem for you with this. That's what I'm going to do."

Anathea winced and took a step back. "Brace, please don't."

"But it'll be amazing! I've got the power of the Muse at my fingertips. It'll be something worthy of you, with her help!"

"That thing hasn't written a single word itself, has it? You've been writing. It may ease some of your frustrations but you haven't mentioned it levitating in the night and writing entire manuscripts by itself."

"What difference does that make? I mean, this is clearly an endorsement of hers. I must have something in me that she sees as worthy of her vision. Why else would I have ended up with this thing? I'm practically obligated to write. Why wouldn't you want a poem of your own?"

"First of all, because you seem to be trusting the Muse to write it for you instead of yourself, if I'm reading this right. You have a magic quill. That's grand, but why does it mean there's some special mission behind it? Why does it have to be me?"

Brace darkened. "If I were to write it with some other quill, would that be better?"

"Still no. Brace, I'm not one for poetry. I'm logic and reason and science and formulaic magic. I have no need for poetry. I think it would be better spent writing such epics for others."

Brace sighed. He tucked the quill into his pocket. "Well, it's not like anything I've ever written ever got me the girl anyway. This shouldn't be different."

Anathea stepped up to him and snapped her fingers in his face. He looked up at her. "That's the problem. You're not writing this to be a gift to me. You're writing this for your own reasons. You're thinking now if you could find the right verse you're going to unlock my heart and I'll be falling into your arms, don't you? I am fully aware of how attracted you are to me, Brace. But what's the point of this? Do you think if you shove gifts at me I can be bought? If you find the right magic word or pricey bauble or pick up line, I'm just going to melt?"

He stood up and walked away from her, hands in the air. "Okay, okay, okay! Don't rub it in. I'm sorry. No magic poetry for you. I get it."

"Do you understand why? Are you listening to me?"

"So I find you appealing. Sue me. Everyone does. I thought dedicating some verse to you would be a worthy thing."

"If not for the motive behind it, maybe it would be. Come on, Brace. I learned to read humans well. Your men and many inclined women dogged me throughout my journey to Spiral. In Halvertown, young men drew pictures of their anatomy and sent them to me with their addresses. For the record, I'm sure most of those pictures were exaggerated."

"That does sound like Halvertown," he muttered.

"Tell me, Brace, have you ever written poetry or anything else for a woman you fancied without hoping it would land them in bed with you?"

Brace refused to meet her gaze.

"Have you ever conjured up one of those things simply to be a gift? No expectation, no obligation, no false hopes? Can you?"

He sighed again. "Perhaps not."

"Perhaps not. Brace, please. Don't expect to buy women with prizes or poetry. We're smarter than that. My affections aren't something won by transactions. I'm looking for something else."

"What are you looking for, then? What kind of man or elf-man pleases your heart?"

"I didn't come to Spiral to win hearts," she said quickly, and turned away from him. Brace's stomach hollowed. Whatever had brought the elf here, it wasn't to settle down and call any given male her own.

"Forgive me for...well, everything, then. I haven't meant to be a burden."

She fidgeted with her fingers and turned to face him again "Forgive me as well if I'm being harsh. Brace, you could be an incredible friend to me. I just build trust very slowly. I have my reasons. I just don't want false expectations on your part about my inclinations. I don't want you to waste your time scribing words that won't win me. And whatever you do, please don't buy me anything."

"Could I at least buy you a drink at the tavern of your choice when this is over? Maybe some plate of fine cooked food. Maybe we could just, you know, talk."

She smiled. It was the first time he'd seen her light up with real sincerity, and it made his woes melt away. "I think that's a great way to get out friendship off on a good foot. I do need help finding the finest cuisine in Spiral."

He bowed, but stopped partway down. "Hey. Over there. Look.

See what the light's falling on over there?"

Anathea walked over to it and saw a round metal cover bolted down to the floor. It was engraved in Imperial Script, but she saw that it was a warning not to enter. "What is this?"

"That's an access port to the Tubes," he said. He walked over and studied the bolts. "It's a huge underground network of tunnels that we began to dig out after Thurach. These portholes were supposed to be all over Spiral. They were never finished and most of them were sealed off. In theory, we'd use them to get to safety if something attacked the city in force again."

"Can we get where we need to go with the Tubes?"

"They'll definitely get us out of the neighborhood, maybe ahead of the riots." He pulled out his quill again and tested the point against the bolts. It cut through the top of one with no resistance. "You're right, I don't think I could dull this quill. I can cut the bolts apart with this, but it'll take some time."

They heard voices and footsteps in the alleyway. They exchanged silent looks. Anathea went back to dragging flagons in front of the door, while Brace worked at cutting the bolts away with the quill. There were three bolts, but cutting at them diagonally from the top ensured he could slice them in half and free the cover. The quill cut through the top of the porthole cover easily. It even seemed that the quill was cutting wider swaths than its tip should have allowed.

He had no plans to complain.

They heard a doorway on the other side of the alley crash open.

"They must know we're hiding out in the area," Anathea hissed. "Cut faster!'

"I'm not exactly singing an opera over here." He finished the first bolt and went to the second.

Boom boom boom. The rioters were pounding on the stairwell door. They saw torches flickering. Brace cursed and cut faster.

Anathea took a position between Brace and the door, warming her hands with more defensive magic.

"Come on, come on, come one," she said.

The door crashed open as Brace finished the second bolt. Anathea threw a focused burst of golden light at the rioters as they came in, throwing two of them against the walls hard enough to knock them out.

Their torches fell. Anathea extinguished them with a pass of her hands. "Any time, Brace!"

Three more came through the doorway. She heard more of them coming downstairs from inside the house.

One of them threw a torch at Anathea. She sidestepped it, caught it and threw it back, blowing the palm of her hand in mid air. It exploded in a blinding flash, lighting two of the rioters on fire and knocking one backward out the door. They screamed and batted at the flames eating their clothes.

"Got it!" Brace tucked the quill in his jacket and pulled on the porthole cover. It squealed backward on rusty hinges. "Go, go, go!"

Anathea ran, jumped and slid over the dinner table, and then over to Brace. "Looks like a drop. I'll go first and levitate you down."

She jumped and floated into the darkness.

Brace heard it before he saw it. The man from the doorway was running at him. He launched himself at Brace as he looked up to track the sound.

He punched Brace in the face twice, then pounded him time and again in the chest and stomach. Brace tasted blood.

"No getaway for you, lad," the attacker snarled. "The elf is ours."

Brace saw that no one remained to help his attacker. "Nobody's left to help you," he wheezed, and coughed out some blood.

When the attacker pinned him against the wall by his throat and stopped to look around, Brace drew the quill again and cut through the attacker's wrist. He screamed and backed away, clutching his wounded limb. He sliced the man across the face, then shoved him into the dining table.

He heard Anathea calling for him. He was glad she went first. It would probably be easier for her to levitate him without having to fend off attackers. At least, that's what she said, wasn't it? He hoped he was remembering it right.

There was a twenty foot drop through the porthole. The wooden ladder that had been set there once had rotted away to twigs. All he could do was hope.

He stumbled to the porthole and fell headfirst into the dark. *I have faith,* he thought. *Catch me, Anathea...*

"It is said the goddess does not befriend easily. For all of her charms, she stays aloof because past a certain point, she can't relate to human concerns anymore. It is said she doesn't want to hurt when we age and die, for with her passions, such wounds heal slowly at best. Given what's described of her at the temple, though, I could guess that when she does befriend, she is the most loyal and warmhearted of companions, fierce in her loyalty and steady in her faith. I've taken that as an instruction manual for my own life."

- Edwin Falls, curator of the Hanging Museum, central Spiral

Grandmother's Tavern had yet to be touched by the riots, but the discontent was coming. Four people were in the tavern where dozens usually mingled: Granny herself, the heavyset old woman who owned the place and ran the bar, who was wiping down mugs; Spuds, her slow on the draw grandson who was regardless an excellent cook; a gliphid named Tressa who stayed next to the window panes, looking up and down the street for any sign of danger; and Valen, the sole customer spending ring coins tonight.

Valen was a swashbuckler by nature, or at the very least, he dressed the part. He stood at six foot six, but hunched his broad shoulders over a table with two tall, empty mugs on it. His mane of black hair was shot with gray, especially at the temples, and it hung in disarray about his shoulders. His beard was neatly trimmed, thin streaks of hair from ear to jaw likewise peppered pale. Tonight he wore a black shirt, a black leather vest, and black pants with brown boots. He'd have worn black boots, but a man's got a budget to consider.

Not that one would know from his drinking habits. "Tressa?" He asked, voice deep, "Two more, please? I can still feel my toes."

The gliphid snaked her view up and down the street one more time, four sets of hands bracing her against the window glass. She turned with a sigh, breath fogging the window as she trotted to the bar. Usually, Tressa was a good conversationalist. Valen saw fit not to worry her. He wasn't drinking because things were going well, after all.

Then, he swore his fortunes changed. *She* walked into the bar, and what a *she* this was! She was clearly a muse, and quite possibly the most impossibly beautiful woman he'd ever seen. Everything about her was daydream perfect, and her virtually nonexistent attire didn't disappoint, either. Her mane of fine brown hair fell down almost to mid-back, but it stirred in the breeze outside as she came in, blue eyes falling upon him, lips slightly parted but turning into a smirk.

He thought he smiled. He might have actually blushed. He stood up a little straighter and tried his famous devil's smile, with one charming eyebrow arched for effect.

She walked over to him with no pretension and laid her hand upon the table. "I've been looking for you."

"I've been dreaming of you," he said, and his mouth spread into a stupid, toothy grin. "I might have had a bit to drink. So confirm for me, you're standing there, right? Muse of the Temple?"

"You could say that." She brushed some stray hair away from her face. "What if I told you that we're old friends? Suppose I said you were my best friend in any world, and right now I need you?"

"Lady, I'll be any friend you ever need if you but stand there and let my eyes worship you forever."

She laughed. "You used that line on me when we first met. But I doubt you remember that."

The muse of the temple sat down and scooted her chair in. Valen would mourn the loss of the view but there was no part of her that wasn't flawless to behold. "How much do you know about the religion of Anastasia the Muse?"

"Are you going to try to convert me? I was great at finger painting when I was a kid. I made a giant snail my father thought was a mean spirited boulder."

"Just humor me, friend. Do you know the legend of the Sleepers?"

"Vaguely. But I like your voice. So, do tell it to me."

Tressa dropped off two more beers and then hurried to the window again.

Valen pushed a beer to Anastasia. "Sorry. She's really worried about things going bad this way. She should have asked you for an order. Have one of mine. I mean, do you want it? Maybe you do finer wines or something?"

"Thank you." She took the large mug, dwarfing her hand as she lifted it, and chugged the entire contents in one breath. Valen counted what must have been twenty gulps. Granny leaned over the bar and stared.

"This stuff doesn't phase me if I don't want it to," the Muse said, gently setting it down, "I do know the good stuff when I taste it. When all of this is over I'm going to come here with my tolerances turned off and knock back ten of these. You watch me."

Valen's mouth hung wide open. "Well….that….happened."

"Sleepers?" she prodded.

"Oh, well, that. Scholars think that Anastasia is a member of an entire race of gods and goddesses. They say some of these beings can wrap themselves up in a mortal lifetime and sleep in the back of a mortal mind, human in every way but asleep at the reigns, so to speak. These Sleepers are sometimes the most creative and intelligent people of a generation, because they can't help but stand out even in their mortal life-dreams. I've heard it said that it's all, you know, a metaphor. That it means there's potentially a sleeping god or goddess in all of us that waits to be awakened. That sort of thing. Inspirational talk."

"You sound skeptical."

"I'm not out rioting over 'Anastasia has forsaken us' or 'we demand whatever.' Or whatever it is now. I think the riots have taken a life of their own. Most of it was started by die hard faithfuls who took a kick in the balls and couldn't handle it. Religious types always seem so close to a frenzy any given day as it is. That's why I never got on board."

"You don't think it's being incited by the so-called 'Mindful?'"

"Never trust a bitter skeptic. They're just as bad. No one's hands are clean at this point."

Valen took a few sips from his mug as Anastasia studied him. She seemed to be waiting for something. She chewed her lip and blinked rapidly, then looked down at her hands.

"Look, I've got a mug in my head," he said, using the common phrase that meant he was too drunk to think straight. "You're the most beautiful anything I've ever seen in whatever and I'll talk to you over a hundred dawns, but I'll be a lot better if I can get a hold of where all of this is going."

"Hand," she said, holding out her own. He stared at it like a serpent for a moment, then reached out and lightly took it. She closed her fingers and trapped his palm in warmth. She rubbed it with her other hand. "Is this a good life for you? Have you done great things?"

He was remarkably sober now, and he didn't know why. He suddenly wanted to talk to her, tell her everything she'd ever want to know. He felt a strange trust now, that this was someone safe and wise. How did he know this? When she'd walked in, all he thought about was how great the night would be if he could score *that* prize. Now, he stilled his mind and let the gravity of the moment in, and he looked into her eyes now as though she was his most important confessor.

"I've made my share of mistakes. Sometimes I hurt people. I was young and I wasn't always aware of myself. I've learned from that. I've tried to grow. I don't have the swagger of my youth anymore and I no longer try to overpower people. I don't think myself ultimately right or the most important person in the room anymore. I've learned much and I've tried to live a life that expounds on that learning. I have tried to be still and without judgment and I've tried to be good wherever I can be, but I'm lonely. Lonely beyond all measure."

He looked away from a moment. Where had all of that come from? Why did that feel so accurate? Why tell this muse in her skimpy bikini-thing anything at all? That wasn't the direction he wanted. Charm, glitz, glamour her into laughter and booze, wasn't that the game plan? Wasn't it usually? Why did his voice sound so far away?

"You had so much swagger before," she smiled, but her eyes cried without moisture. "I always loved that about you. You were confident and you spoke your mind, but spoke it well. Never a wasted word from you."

He tried to pull his hand back. "Who are you? What are you trying to do to me?"

"The Sleepers are real. There are so many of them. Amaranthines, that's what we're called. You see, sometimes the monotony of eternity gets to be too much to bear. We wrap ourselves in mortal lives and fall asleep in the back of their minds, just like you said. We forget ourselves completely. The life we lead, from birth to death, with all of those mortal experiences, it's the one thing that can leave permanent changes to our immortal nature. It can change us when we emerge again. It's how immortals can transform themselves."

He stared at her. Something nagged at his mind. At the seat of his mind, at the core of it in the deepest part of is brain, it was struggling in chains he never knew could bind it. He just stared, fully still.

"Except, it's not a perfect process. Sometimes the Sleeper manifests his or her powers subconsciously as the Amaranthine within reacts to the mortal life-dream. Sometimes, rare times, the Sleeper becomes lucid, fully aware of the Amaranthine in their mind. Their consciousness merges with the sleeper and they understand everything from inside a mortal coil. Sera'loq, that's a very good friend to us both, he does that all the time. He's always waking up inside his Sleeper lives." She giggled. "Drives him batty, too."

His skin paled. He hung his head, eyes going wild, darting back and forth, confronting a flood of memories that came pouring out of a hidden place. He braced himself with his arms on the table, then lowered his forehead onto his arms. Anastasia dimmed. It was happening.

She reached over the table and gently ran her fingers through his hair. Nobody else noticed. Granny was in the back room telling her grandson about the beer chugging muse, and Tressa was watching the windows.

After a long time, Valen lifted his head slightly from his arms. "Tressa," he said, and his voice had changed. Anastasia knew this accent. "Three more beers and one for the muse, quickly. Don't worry about the riots. They're no longer a threat to you here."

He sat up now and looked at Anastasia. Even though this was a mortal form looking at her, she knew the body language perfectly. Every tick, every blink, everything.

"I'm sorry," she said quietly, and heaved a heavy breath. "I know you needed the Sleep."

"Hand," he said, and when she gave it, he closed his hands over it in such a familiar way. "I told you to wake me if you ever needed me. I told you. You're not wounding me. You're doing what I asked."

She got up and hugged him. He stood up and hugged her back. They were holding each other when Tressa dropped off the mugs, rolled her eyes and walked away.

"Michael's turned against us," she said softly into his ear. "He went to Sleep after you did, but he had a bad life and came to a violent end. He came out of it as...well, he's taken the title 'Lord of Ten Shadows.'"

Valen stepped back and stared, skin pale. "You've got to be kidding me," he gasped.

"No. He goes by the name 'Philosopher' now. It's something that someone he loved called him in that life-dream, and he took it sarcastically. Michael, as we knew him, is gone. He is Philosopher, the Lord of Ten Shadows. Right out of Sera'loq's devil myth."

Valen parted from her and took two shaky steps. He braced himself against the back of the chair with one hand. "How bad is it?"

"Persephone had to stop him from wiping out millions of lives in the Primary Duality. He wanted to return mortals to a baseline that could be remade according to his plan. He thought if something horrible enough happened, people would have to depend on each other again and the old plan would be right back on track."

He stared at her, mouth agape, eyes frozen.

"He's changed physically, too. You should see him in his Amaranthine form. Snow white skin, cold blue eyes, everything is black leather and metal. His wings are black and edged in gray. But his eyes, that's the thing. They are so, so cold now, so unfeeling. I don't know him when I look into them."

He massaged his face. "I thought you'd wake me if the Shei'oshans returned, or something like that. I'm...I'm utterly terrified."

She turned him toward her and laid a hand on his chest. " He's cut me off from most of my power and he let my people see me. You know we're not meant to be seen. He's trying to make a point about how toxic we are to our following if they know we're real. These riots are the result."

"So, that's it. Michael...pardon me, Philosopher's head games." He took her shoulders. "You know we're not a match for him. The things I saw him do before...All of us together couldn't bring him down if we wanted to."

Anastasia hung her head. "That's why I need you. I don't know what to do next. I'm still far above anything mortal, probably above any Sleeper, but I'm much diminished according to our terms. I'm just having a crisis of faith. I don't know what to do for my people right now. I'd go before them and tell them to stop, but that would just breed the same hardcore zealotry we've always wanted to avoid, wouldn't it? They'd lose all free will bending themselves to my favor and they'd start to hate anyone that I seemed to favor. I can't interact with them directly and not make it worse. I mean, that's right, isn't it?"

"Well, I sure as Hell can, can't I? That much I can do. You leave that to me. I'll go out into the crowd and start shutting down the riots here and there. Might take a bit, but I can start working counter to the riots. I have a feeling I can persuade them."

"Would you? I'll see if I can find Philosopher and derail him somehow."

"I'd be happy to. Let me ask you this, though. Have you considered the logistics of appealing to your people directly instead of hiding from them? You seem so convinced that being blatant is bad."

"Knowing what it would cost them?"

"Respectfully, it's what you've been trained to think it would cost them. You're not even trying to mold them aright. The carriage jumped the curb and you've already given up on trying to steer it back. Why are you resisting this so much? Who else would they listen to?"

Anastasia rubbed her mouth with one hand. "I'm scared. You're right, I've been trained to think that the consequences are absolute. It does make perfect sense. I'm afraid I'll destroy everything that was beautiful about this place and this world if I accept my place as a certainty in it."

"Frankly, he's already proven your certainty. While you refuse to do so, Philosopher's riots are tearing Spiral down. This city needs you to put away your self-doubt."

"Easier said than done!"

"No. As easy as I said, it's done. You've lived among them for millennia as a whisper over their shoulder. My advice is to take your place."

She crossed her arms. "I'm starting to regret waking you."

"Liar." He leaned in and kissed her forehead. "No one has ever been the counsel for you that I have been. You've said that time and again. I'm sorry if it isn't what you want to hear, but if anything's clear, the old days of Spiral are gone. You need to take it into the new days personally. At this point, there isn't much left to lose."

Anastasia took a long, deep breath. "I'll think about it."

"Meanwhile, I'll go take care of your riots. After I stop by a store down the way and trade out some of this. I need to feel more like me in this skin. Speaking of, love your new look! Wasn't I smitten with you enough before? You sadist."

She smiled and rested her forehead against his. "Thank you, dear friend."

"As I've always been."

He dropped some ring coins on the table and went out the door. Anastasia took a moment to chug the beers, to the horror of Granny and Tressa.

"Where does mister Valen find these women?" Granny muttered.

"His name isn't mister Valen, and I'm no average woman." She stuck out her tongue and left.

Finding himself reawakened to divinity, Valen found his budget much relaxed and spent his ring-coins accordingly.

Valen slung a wide cloak of wolf's fur around his shoulders. It nearly closed in the front. He now wore a black leather vest with no shirt beneath, flaunting his strong pectorals. He had loose black trousers now tucked into knee high black boots, and a gold earring in his left ear. He was testing the weight of a long, redwood handled hammer with a stone head. It was said to be too large to lift properly, and the shopkeeper gawked at Valen's light fingers with the weapon.

A mass of ring-coins stood in front of the shopkeep. He wasn't complaining. Valen had come in saying that some rioters had parted with them as a donation. He didn't ask questions.

"Ah, one more thing. That gauntlet, there? The metal one, the silver one with the engraving. That one."

"Just the one, sir?"

Valen nodded with a wide smile. The shopkeeper took it off its mount behind him and gave it over. Valen slid it on and fastened it down. It was an elegant showpiece with little martial value, but he loved it. It was engraved with swirls and knots. Metal closed over his hand and fingers, sculpted to resemble fingernails at the end. The skin of his palm beneath was still bare.

"Much better," he said, flexing his hands. "Symbolism, you know."

"Is that all, mister Valen?"

"No more Valen. I've had a change of heart. Call me Tyr. Tyr of the North."

"**Civilization began when two people saw a painting on a cave wall and instead of fighting each other, they talked about art.**"

- **Queen Ilesa Ronmacharte**

King Ronmacharte rubbed his temples.

The throne room had long been a wonder of Spiral. Over two hundred feet wide and perfectly round, it had a transparent floor running the span through which visitors could view a detailed model of the city of Spiral. The model had taken over a hundred sculptors months to craft, and a team of engineers had labored long on the mechanism supporting the model city so it could turn ever so slowly beneath the floor. The King's throne was on the far end of the room but the bookshelves behind it and flanking it were empty. The roof was a galaxy of miniscule lights set into a painted sky, recreating the nighttime of Spiral down to the constellations above.

However, the shouting echoing off the throne room walls was hardly a masterpiece. Ronmacharte leaned forward and covered his face with his hand as it continued.

It was his daughter, Petrenella. He regretted naming her something more fitting, like Petulanta or something. The fifteen year old girl had barged into his private meeting with Cappus, wielding her mother's temper. Her fiery red hair was tied back, and her gold and white dress left only her hands and head uncovered. It was monogrammed with the royal R of the Ronmacharte family.

"You can't seriously be turning your back on Spiral!" she wailed. "We should be out there doing something, not hiding in the palace!"

"The guardsmen outside the palace are being overwhelmed. We can't deploy our military assets against our own people without betraying our conditions of government. My family swore never to raise a hand to Spiral's people. My hands are tied."

"Your hands aren't tied! Get out there and lead your people! Shout from horseback in full plate if you have to, but don't just hole up in here and leave them to their fate!"

The King shot a look to Cappus. "Cappus, summarize the briefing you've given me."

Cappus turned toward the Princess and cleared his throat, his staff coming to rest on the glass floor with a shallow tap. "We estimate that more than sixty percent of Spiral is rioting now. There are further edges of the city still under control, however. The property damage is extensive and our guardsmen are outnumbered twenty to one in some areas. Those guardsman who themselves did not feel the apocalypse is nigh and started rioting themselves, of course."

"That's my point," The Princess said. "You need to be taking the city back, not hiding in your palace!"

The King waved her off. Petrenella, please. We haven't had an emergency of this scale in Spiral in our lifetimes. The guardsmen are accustomed to a good life. They only have so much experience dealing with this. Of course they're going to be overwhelmed. Spiral is going to have to burn itself out. The best thing I can do now is safeguard my palace and my family, and then deal with the aftermath when the smoke clears."

Cappus tapped his staff for attention and said, "This is just as I advised you once, your highness. If you would have pliant women, forbid them to read. We know your daughter has secreted books away from the vault below. Undoubtedly those subversive texts have rendered her rebellious."

Petrenella's face reddened. She turned on Cappus. "That's the problem you two have created in Spiral! The people aren't free. They're sedated. You forbid them anything that can incite them to think for themselves. Instead, you pour the same thing down their throats every day about Spiral being a paradise and how lucky they

132

are to live here, and you take away anything they might encounter that teaches them otherwise! You're doing this because you're afraid of being criticized!"

She turned to her father. "I imagine your court would be difficult to lead if you had a council of magical free-thinkers questioning your every move. You keep Formulaic Magic as a noble's right while forbidding Creative Magic to everyone else. Now do you see what you've bred? A vast lynch mob incapable of empathy."

The King stood up and marched toward his daughter. She shrank away at first but held his gaze. "You think it's better that the people of Spiral should throw fireballs at each other right now? You think it better if they can crush a building or slay their neighbors out of hand?"

"You've also taken away their ability to defend themselves! How many would-be wizards out there are powerless to save their families right now? How many of them can heal and repair the damage done to our city? If you haven't noticed, father, the crowd's doing fine tearing it all done without any magic at all. All they had to see was that the Muse was real and to see her thrown down from on high. Now they're inconsolable!"

"Yes, the subject of the Muse! I saw her in person. So did Cappus. We were all but spanked and sent back to the palace to await her word. Do you think I outrank a goddess? She told me to wait. Why isn't she more involved in stopping all of this? She could. A wave of her hand could do anything, or so we're told. Still, the riots power on and my people end up in graves. Where is your beloved Muse now?"

Petrenella's eyes shifted. The bold glint softened into a wound. Her bottom lip quivered and she looked away.

"There you have it," her father said. "You've long wanted to be a muse of the temple and we've forbidden it at every turn. As if I would allow my daughter to be one of *those* women. Virtually skyclad and flirting with random lowborn artists in the streets like you're doing a service to humanity. Now, look at your paragon. All of this has simply proven why the safeguards we established were the right thing to do."

"I'm never going to believe that. What's more, I love the muses. You don't understand them. They wander the city and counsel people about everything. They're pillars of the community. They sing and dance and bring joy to everyone. They bring peace and goodwill, and they entice artists to create art of every kind. I want to be part of that! I don't want to be stuffed in my room in a locked down palace watching the world fall apart from on high. I want to be someone who finds the beauty in people. They're not what you think they are!"

"They are attention seeking whores, and their goddess an irresponsible, absentee landlord at best. I obey her because it's clear I'm outmatched and with the people, outranked by her word. Don't go thinking the display of power she showed us stays us, however. We can see how invested she is in the fate of spiral with her inaction. She's probably doting over some muscular, scantily clad male somewhere and not bothering with the rest of us. Too inconvenient."

Petrenella opened her mouth to speak but her father snapped a finger up to point at her nose. She bit back her response. "I will have no further argument on the matter. The subject is closed. Go back to your room and when you get there, get all of the books off of your bed and out from under it and have the guards put them back in the vault. If I find you down there again I'll see you're properly imprisoned for it. I'll shake these worthless romantic notions of yours out of your head, one way or another."

"I've studied everything I can get my hands on about the muses, father. Their ideas, beliefs, techniques, their history. I *am* a muse in all but official name, and you can't take that away from me. I'm going to get out of this palace eventually, I'm going to join the temple, and I'm going to heal the world in the best way possible. I'm sorry you choose not to be part of that."

"If you leave this palace without my permission, you will be leave your name behind. I will openly disown you and have you removed from succession for the throne. If you insist on cavorting about with the great unwashed, so be it, but you will lose any connection to this family doing it."

"Some things are bigger than family, father. Like the fate of the world." She spun on one heel and strode out of the chamber without looking back. The guards closed the blue marble double doors leading into the chamber behind her.

"She has her mother's will," the King said. "I'm not sure I favor that."

"She would make for an unstable queen, my lord, that much is obvious." Cappus smoothed out his robe and adjust his grip on his staff. "As for the Muse, we are best served biding our time until we see how she commits to things. As it is, our hands are legally tied. Between safeguarding the royal family and securing the immediate neighborhoods around Spiral, the best we can do is wait for the riots to slow of their own accord."

"At least we're conserving our resources." He cracked his knuckles, a tick Cappus knew meant the King was upset. "She'll learn someday how important our decisions have been."

Petrenella was a reader. This meant she was prepared.

She had been smuggling her favorite books out of the castle to an Inn elsewhere in Spiral for some time now, along with a change of clothes and a room rented with no questions asked over the long term. She had saved her allowance for some time and used it to easily bribe the guards, several of whom had known her long enough to have played with her as a toddler - and whose ears she had bent against the King's decisions over time with clever oratory. Their loyalty to her was unquestionable.

Still, she sniffled as she changed into a white long sleeved shirt and loose, high waisted pants. She pulled her knee length black boots on with blurry eyes. A father was a father. Nobody hated their fights more than she did. And that Cappus! Ooooh, the things he said! This was a wizard?

It would take her about 45 minutes to make it to the Inn. It was on the edge of control against the riots, but she needed only concern herself with staying mostly unseen. She pulled on a cloak made of blue felt with a butterfly sewn onto the back. One quick pull and the hood obscured her so completely that only looking at her from underneath would show her face.

Her garden - she would miss that. She loved reading in her garden. It gave her pause and she almost stopped. She was moments away from calling it all off and just hiding in her room a while longer. Then again, the temple was said to have some of the most beautiful gardens in Spiral. She could always do some reading there if she got permission.

So then, onward. That was the only course now. She nodded to herself and continued to get ready.

She would send her father letters, to be sure. She still loved the man, even after fits like this. A daughter could not just abandon her father without better cause, she reasoned. A daughter also could not put off her dreams for anyone that dared to hold her back.

In her mind, she saw the path to Anastasia's temple and with a deep breath, she set out to start a new life.

> **"Your eye dimmed when you looked at me.**
> **The oceans dried. The moon fell. The sun wept.**
> **Where once was love, indifference reigned**
> **and all love and laughter were barren.**
> **I dreamt of words to heal you,**
> **I dreamt of ways to steal you,**
> **But you turned away, wore silence as a cloak.**
> **You whom I loved so dear, I never knew again.**
> **- "Passing," Alaso Malutt, Scribe of the King**

Anastasia couldn't help but smile. Even as she made her way through the chaos, occasionally willing a broken window to mend itself or healing the fallen in the streets, she felt warmer than she had before.

Good ol' Tyr. Long had he coveted her, true, but in his character it had tempered a loyal friend and confidant who had been her anchor through many crises over the centuries. For all of his swagger and war-hewn skills, his word was unshakable and his bond to her true.

Decades ago, he had come to her and said that he was done with his long span of consciousness and needed Sleep. He wanted to wake up new. He wanted to wake up not so eager toward bravado and more inclined for peace of mind. Anastasia knew that part of this dealt with her. He knew that his womanizing ways in a past life had put her off, and his confidence was too overblown to be reasonable at times. She knew this was partly to make himself a better choice for her, though at that time, she wouldn't have dreamed of parting ways from Michael.

But then, Michael had parted ways from her, Slept, and become the thing hounding her today. She reminded herself that relationships had been justifiably ended for less, where the ongoing destruction of an entire city just to teach her a lesson was considered. Truth be told, Tyr's loyalty had touched her in the past. Perhaps it was time to reassess him...

She walked across a street where people were fleeing from rioters. Some walked, some trotted at a good pace. None of them saw her. Not that it mattered now. Even if they could, they had concerns beyond some beautiful human woman walking in the road. She heard breaking glass and smelled burning wood. She sighed and her eyes moistened.

She was known to be the most emotional of the Amaranthines. She always wore her emotions openly, even blatantly. She never felt put off by this. In her mind, it was what she was meant for. If raw emotion offended, good or bad, then she was not the person to have around. She accepted her raw state.

Not so much now, though. She felt she had cried too much even for her circumstance. She began to doubt. She felt the shadow crawling across her heart. For the first time since she had created this world and nursed it into her current form, she felt poisonous to it. There was no recourse she could think of.

Through all of this, Tyr's words circled her mind. Could he be right? Was the answer to resolving all of this right in front of her?

Then, she saw him, standing in the middle of the next street. He had taken a more human form as well, doubtless in mockery of her.

He wore a long black coat and a black and gray gentleman's waistcoat, buttoned up with silver buttons. He wore a purple cravat with a silver stone in the center, black loose fitting slacks, and black heeled boots. His hair matched the color of his outfit but was tied back in a ponytail. His skin hinted at a human color but remained deathly pale, while his blue eyes were absent their subtle glow.

He stood there in the chaos of the street, hands folded in front of him, watching her with a blank expression. The rioting around him was intensifying even as she watched, and she wondered if this was his doing or more consequences unfolding from what was already done.

She marched up to him, making no attempt to hide her broken spirit.

"This is what you've done to me," she hissed at him. "Are you happy? Am I humble enough for the great Philosopher now?"

When he spoke now, it was a deep voiced whisper that still managed to be easily heard. "I take no pleasure in this, be assured. But a point had to be made."

"Damn you and your precious point!" she screamed in his face. The world did not notice. "You wrecked my Eden and I'll never forgive you for this!"

"How long do you think you could sustain this world? Do you think your endless worship is any different than what the Great Enemy takes for himself? We never should have troubled humanity, Anastasia. We were wrong. We were always wrong. We had the hubris to believe we could rule over mortals and escort them to our divinity but we were too much like them in the end. Our society paid the price. Now, every one of you with your own secret worlds accomplishes little more than to repeat the sin of overwatch on millions of people of your own. You all say you encourage free will even while you whisper destinies into mortal ears and direct them as your whims allow."

He turned to look down the street. A flying glass bottle shattered against his face. He failed to acknowledge it with the slightest twitch. It left no telling mark. He swirled a finger and the bottle reassembled itself and floated before him, seamless as if it had never broken.

"How do we justify the righteousness of our cause while we lord over worlds as their ultimate beings? Does that not run contrary to everything we ever embraced about free will? Perhaps with age we can see our folly and undo it. I now dream of a reality, all realities, being free of our kind's influence. Mortals everywhere must be allowed to determine their own destinies without our smallest whisper."

Anastasia clapped slowly. "Lovely speech, but you're a bit dry on your delivery. Color me unimpressed. I've allowed my world to progress entirely on its own. I've prevented no misfortunes. I occasionally create and perform art, or inspire my people do the same. They love me and I love them. We revel together in the beauty of life. Ours is a relationship built on joy and revels. Only something as cynical as you are would imagine it was toxic. You misled yourself so much you even attacked me. *Me.*"

Anastasia slapped him across the face with all of her strength. To her credit, it struck him well, and he even turned his head with the blow. The windows blew out for three blocks around and the people scurried for cover without realizing why.

"As if I've been nothing to you for thousands of years," she snarled at him, eyes cruel. Her voice started low but continued to build into a shout. "I've been there to comfort you in your darkest moments and you've allowed me to bring you back from them! I've been there when no one else was to dry your tears and hold your shoulders when you sobbed for humanity. I was there to defend you against other Amaranthines who thought you were too dangerous to survive when you awoke last. I wept when you left me to Sleep in a mortal life and change into this thing you are now. And what comes as my thanks? You attack me, poison my people's minds, and provoke waves of violence in a peaceful city because *your precious agenda* is more important than the human lives we were created to shepherd!"

She stabbed a finger at the street. "None of this happened without you, so you are the cause. All you've proven to me as that you are no better than your oh-so-terrifying Great Enemy anymore! These are his tactics. You've said this is how he *feeds.* All the dead and wounded in this city have you to thank for overlooking them as living things when your chess game with the past became your only concern!"

Philosopher turned his back to her but listened. The street was empty now. He let the bottle drop and break again.

"I had to become like him to destroy him," he said at last. "There was no choice. The other side of me, the...kinder side as it pleases you, had not the power or the mind to engineer his fall."

"I'm not going to have this argument with you again. You can't change my mind. I know I've bent the rules a lot, but how could anyone expect me to ignore my own people? You broke your own laws when you saved me from those men! Haven't we had enough hypocrisy already?"

"I wish I could take all of this back, Anastasia, but there is no way around it." He turned to face her again. His eyes were slightly softer, but still carried a cold detachment. "We have been and always will be bad for mortals. We can't escape it. If you love them, abandon them. Let them throw down your name and your faith. Let them truly self-determine. Let reason rule them."

"I love them too much." Her voice cracked. She hung her head. "I won't let go of my world. I've never been happier in thousands of years than I have been here as their patron spirit. My love for what I have here will weather me against losing even you. I have meaning and purpose. I believe in my calling. I believe in my hands and my wit and my passion. I don't believe in you anymore. I can't."

He shook his head. "Then this thing must play out its course."

She stepped up to him and grabbed his lapel. "Give me my powers back, you son of a bitch. Then leave this world. Leave it forever and don't trouble me with your holy cause ever again. I'd rather be quit of you in mind forever than be made to suffer your every sadistic whim."

"All things in due time, Anastasia."

"Where's Sera'loq? Where's Zodiac and Persephone? Would they stand for this?"

In his awkward silence, she divined the truth.

She took a step back, mouth wide open. "You're...doing this to *all of us?*"

"This very moment," he said quietly. "To teach you all about waste."

For the first time in in their history, she stared at him in true disbelief. This thing before her was alien now. This thing that had once been the kindest and warmest of all the Amaranthines had finally gone mad. This magnificent being she had made love to in the heart of lightning storms, at the bottom of oceans, in the explosions of volcanoes and the glittering surface of comets was beyond being called truly humane now. The very thought of touching him sent poison racing under her skin.

Unable to form words, she stumbled away from him, then ran. She held her eyes and sobbed as her heart pulverized into a fine glass dust. He was doing this to all of them! All of them!

She quietly begged the sky for Sera'loq to hear her, or Zodiac, Persephone, Heru, any of them. So many times she reminded them that he was the oldest and most powerful, to put aside judgment and listen, this was such an important cause. Oh, the shame of it all now. The heart searing *shame*.

What they must think of her now as their own worlds turned against them. What if her beloved circle hated her now? Did they blame her for all of this? Could they simply be ignoring her? Oh, and their people. If this was happening on their worlds, how fast would they remember her quick defense of the Amaranthine that ultimately did it to them?

She went deep into the riots of Spiral, now hoping she was so weak the people would see her, turn on her, and kill her. There was nothing she hated more in that moment than the idea of "Anastasia the Muse."

"**For the Hearts of Spiral!**"

- **Popular toast**

Anathea held Brace under one arm while shining light down the Tubes with the other. The round halls curved out of sight in the darkness.

She turned and shined her gem down the way they came. It momentarily brightened into searchlight intensity. No one followed. Their point of entry laid far behind.

With a heavy breath, she let Brace down against the curving wall of the tunnel and traced her fingers along the crystal embedded in her left hand. White lines followed her finger beneath the surface of the gem. One tap, and it activated a new spell with a white starburst.

She waved her palm over Brace's body, watching the shifting white designs on the gem. She held her right hand over his body in different places, channeling healing energy into him with soft blue pulses. The light to see by had shifted to emit from the centermost gem on her chest.

Satisfied, she stood back up, the healing and analysis spells flickering out. "I'm going to have to leave you here for a few minutes while I go look ahead. Just stay here and don't go wandering off."

Brace nodded. Strength was returning to him. His attacker had done real harm, but the elf had tended to that. It tingled where she had worked but he could feel no pain. His body was smoothing out the aftermath of the spell. While the healer had performed her craft well enough, he needed rest.

Anathea traced a different pattern onto her hand gems, then tapped. Two glowing flames appeared in the palms of her hands.

She lowered one to sit next to Brace, then turned with her own torch to go further down the hall. "That'll keep you lit." She wandered off without another word.

Brace struggled to sit up in a better posture beside this strange, flaming thing hovering in the air just beside him. His mind stabilized and he immediately regretted letting Anathea out of his sight.

A pair of blue eyes opened in the darkness near him. Even if Brace had been looking in their direction, he would never have seen them.

"The elf has clever magics," Philosopher said. "I could feel her unique vibration across the span of Spiral."

He was still in his humanized form, having parted ways with Anastasia minutes before. He studied Brace as the pathetic creature panted against the wall, his heart all but shouting for Anathea to return to him. The human couldn't hear a word he said, but deep down in his soul, he felt it. He knew he wasn't alone.

"You are a perfect example of everything I strive not to be," Philosopher said. He walked around Brace, studying him from other angles. "You are so bent by your emotion that you can't reason effectively. The elf is right, you realize. You are feeble. You're doing more to endanger her than to protect her, as you uselessly fantasized."

Brace wiped his eyes and hung his head. Grief blossomed in his chest.

"Don't you miss those moments before you knew her? Perhaps you weren't at your happiest, true. But you weren't compromised. You weren't a broken thing sulking in the dark beneath a city gone mad. How quickly our fortunes change when we learn that special, terrible craving. Our freedom disintegrates and we find ourselves buried in the dark of our own thwarted wants."

Brace brushed the tears away and took a few deep breaths.

"She is a logical, reasonable creature, your precious elf. What room has she for the fiery passions of an artist? Has it occurred to you yet that you've blinded yourself to your own incompatibility? Of course you have. You've imagined a range of scenarios and moments relating how perfectly you think you'll get by if you just open up to each other. The more you draw upon those expectations, the more they'll fail you. You're creating your own distress."

Philosopher paused. "Wait. What is that? The Muse...I sense her on you."

He leaned in close and waved one hand. Brace's leather jacket folded open and Anastasia's wingtip feather jumped into his pale fingers. He stood up and walked away with it, Brace having seen and felt nothing. The feather had a subtle golden glow in the dark, and the tip was blackened by a thin coating of ink.

"Of all the drama, Anastasia. Where are your words of breaking laws now? Whispering we all do, but giving a piece of yourself to this mortal? How contemptible. Your power is still in this feather. If it rejoined you, you might channel back the rest of what I've stolen from you. I suspect you aren't aware of that, my love. Not that you have the power to dispel me in the least, even with it."

He inspected the feather closely. He ran a fingertip through the soft edges.

Immediately a sun burst open in his heart. He remembered Anastasia's powerful, body wracking laugh. He saw her eyes wide with sorrow, tears spilling from the corners and running down her lovely face. He felt her hand passing over his marble-like skin and the passions it stirred within him. He felt her arms around him, her lips on his mouth, kissing with passion that never knew the slightest restraint. She could see a coy bat of the eyelashes and a sexy smirk, and how she would take his hand and lead him to her latest pleasures. He remembered the perfect form of her body and how fearless abandonment of clothes even among other Amaranthines, and how she would stick her tongue out at his smallest reservation.

It ached. His heart suddenly took a dozen wounds.

He flung the feather away. It floated back to Brace behind him and tucked itself back in his jacket, which flipped closed behind it. The goddess had willed that it would never be lost.

Philosopher's hands shifted. Human coloration played across them, especially where he had brushed the goddess' love with his fingertips. It struggled to push further, to race up his arms and draw him back toward humanity, toward emotion.

He balled his hands into fists. He clenched his fingers tight. He grit his teeth and willed it to a halt. He thought of war, famine, pain, disease, death, broken hearts and shattered dreams. He thought of the Great Enemy.

His heart pined for Anastasia. It pulled on her. He stopped it, willed it to be still. He sank to his knees as tears spilled out of his eyes. They floated away against any hint of gravity.

Finally, his skin faded back to a pale white. He had shed his humanized form in a desperate attempt to smother the humanity threatening him. He was in his full Amaranthine form now, but on hands and knees, wings bent. Brace still saw nothing.

Philosopher rose to his feet, slowly at first. *"Even a fragment of the Muse is enough to challenge me,"* he said to himself, his voice returned to its inhuman rumble. *"A mere fragment of her can humble me."*

He considered the implications. *"If it is so easy to dispel me so, I've underestimated my own weaknesses. What have I done? I understand from a point of reason that my actions are correct. Morality and emotion are expendable in the path of success. I believe this. I have to believe this. The stakes are too high for them to be meaningless sacrifices."*

He knew the Great Enemy had no emotion, and that the terrible mind he opposed operated in the coldest reaches of mechanical thought. Feeling was an exploitable weakness and the Great Enemy certainly knew how to exploit tragedy to slow or stop his enemies.

Yet...in those moments he felt warm again from the feather's touch, he felt...strong. A different kind of strength, but strong. He felt his ebbed love and loyalty for the Muse. He felt his angst at betraying her.

"Is what I'm feeling right, or the lingering poison of a weakening emotion?" He let one more tear float out of his eye, but snatched it out of the air with one hand. He watched it dissolve in his palm. *"Without her, I'll never be anything human again."*

He found that even in the darkness, he still regretted it.

Anathea was back, he realized. He turned and saw Anathea pulling brace up again. "I've found a good place to get out. Let's go. Are you better now?"

"I'm fine. I'm having a hard time down here."

"Don't tell me you're afraid of the dark, Brace."

"Don't be silly. The dark's afraid of me, of course."

Philosopher watched them leave, feeling the power of the muse's quill in his jacket. *"Perhaps I am,"* he replied. *"Perhaps I am, at that."*

He had nothing left now but to believe. He couldn't reverse course now. At the very least, his actions sealed his fate. There was no going back. He had to ride through the chain of events to their end.

This time, however, he had a new enemy to contend with:

His own mounting doubt.

"'The Raven Muse,' they called her. Senelle, a muse of the temple who decided that pain was more instructive than inspiration. She crushed hearts, twisted minds, played with people like toys and then wrecked them out of hand, all to produce what she felt was art's only truth: Suffering is the only universal constant. That was a century ago, and people today still wonder if more Raven Muses exist. No proof of this has ever been found and the temple denies them as an urban myth. Of Senelle...no one know what happened to her. We only see in her wake the cost of a broken promise."

- Valer Mohns, court historian to the Ronmacharte family

"Fifteen hundred rings, no less."

The speaker's voice rasped, and the customer who was briefly assigned the name "The Patron" imagined it didn't sound any better when his counterpart was young and healthy. He heard it filtered through a leather mask fit over his nose and mouth, a tube linking it to a burner nearby that sent smouldering herbs into his lungs. A blue healthstone was mounted on the front, glowing in constant exertion as it tried to repair the near-skeletal head with its shock of white hair.

The Patron sputtered, "B-but that piece. It was five hundred yesterday!"

"The mobs weren't as close yesterday. If they close in on this gallery just one more block, I'll burn everything here. No negotiation. You are a buyer or you are not."

The Patron studied the piece in question. It was a large painting showing Anastasia the Muse in her godlike form, clearly taken from the statue at the temple, turning her back on dozens of naked, bleeding, emaciated mortals scrambling for her attention. The Muse looked haughty, waving away the masses with one hand and laughing into a mirror with the other. The painting was drawn in dark pastels, some of it looking smeared on.

"You would burn this? Really? You would throw away all that money?"

"I would deny it to the rioters. I'll not have them keep anything they haven't bought from me personally, and I won't have them sell it where I can't profit. Let's say your donation will help me set up again elsewhere if I can stay ahead of the mob. Not the easiest thing in my condition, but a head start would help. Meaning you only have minutes to decide before I lose my patience."

The Patron licked his lips and kept his eyes fixed on the painting, studying every line. He was dressed in sky blue, the color of nobles in Spiral, but nobody could dress up his obvious greed and self-indulgence. He was heavy from the finest foods, black hair slicked backward over beady eyes, and the cut of his goatee didn't suit his face.

He could probably sell it for two thousand somewhere else, he thought. It would be hard to do, very probably. The city had never seen this private piece and would react poorly to it being shown around without being licensed. That meant moving very carefully if he wanted to sell it on the art underground, but it might be that he could at least score a five hundred ring payout from fencing it.

The curator drew up beside him in the dark room. He was as thin as the desperate souls in the painting, but had no arms. His robes had no sleeve holes and they wrapped tight around his lean body. The robes ended at the knees, revealing his legs to be spindly and his toes shriveled. He walked with great difficulty, wobbling as he went, but somehow balanced. A gliphid wearing black scooted beside him holding his herb burner.

"This piece was painted with the blood of humans mixed in. It's the blood of those believers in the Muse who found their prayers ignored. The frame was wrought from the bones of loved ones they lost when their faith went unanswered. It's a masterpiece of suffering and a statement about the fatalism of believing in gods. One of a kind."

"Who painted it?" The Patron asked.

The curator smiled behind his mask. It lit his dark, shifting eyes. "Trade secret. Fifteen hundred rings. You have two minutes to decide. Or look throughout the rest of my humble gallery. Find something quickly. Time is not on our side and I never take chances."

The Patron ran his fingers over the ring-coins under the leather flap on his belt. The curator watched, breathing labored but otherwise as patient as death.

That's when a woman's voice behind them startled them both. Even the gliphid jumped, scattering some of the herbs in the burner.

"It was painted at his direction," The woman said. She was on the far end of the round gallery. Pillars sculpted to look like young men and women twisting in agony flanked her and circled the room. "This is Savin Durs, if you haven't guessed."

The curator merely nodded once to her. "A muse of the temple. I thought the doors were locked. You have no right to be here. Leave, now."

"I've always considered doors optional, myself."

The curator faced her fully and took a few steps forward. "We have no room for your pretension of wit, muse. See yourself out. If we have need of whores we will contact your temple."

"'Whore' is a word used by men threatened by the term 'goddess.'"

"You have a rather high opinion of yourself. Beautiful you may be, but wanted you are not."

Next to him, the Patron blushed and said nothing, throat dry. This woman was the most poetry perfect beauty he'd ever seen, and her form defied the words of the greatest poets. Something in his hindbrain whispered a warning to his conscious mind, and he knew to keep quiet.

"Beautiful? What do you know about beautiful, Savin? Men say that to me constantly like I've never heard the word before, or it has some godlike power coming from their lips. Do you know beautiful in any meaningful way?"

She walked behind a pillar, and emerged as an older black woman with feline eyes and a seductive curl to her lips. "Can you find beauty in anything other than a surge of hormones? Can you find it in a litter of newborn kittens or a toddler's giggle?"

She disappeared behind another pillar. She emerged again as a heavier oriental woman, a mane of dark hair engulfing her shoulders and her eyes smokey with wit. "I wonder if you can find it clinging to a flower in the morning, glittering in the sun. Can you? Can you find it in a sunrise at all, Savin?"

The Patron paled and took a few steps backward. The curator shot him a cruel glance and then glared anew at Anastasia.

She went behind another pillar, now halfway to them, dragging her fingers along the cold stone that briefly concealed her. She emerged now as a woman of light brown skin in her fifties, full with the form of motherhood. "Savin Durs, I'm every beauty that ever was, and any woman that ever lived. I'm every standard of beauty known to mortals, and standards from worlds removed from this one. I'm the goddess of love and passion and expression. Nothing in the world have I reveled in more than love and beauty."

She went behind another pillar and emerged a pale skinned girl in her late teens, red hair pony tailed back, moving with the fluid steps of a dancer. "This is who I am. I am all of these. I have worn all of these forms at some time or another, sometimes for decades. I've watched love's first spark thousands upon thousands of times and I've wept with every broken heart in the people around me."

One final pillar and she came before them, now wearing the visage she had entered the room with, the pale skinned muse of impossible countenance, brown hair raining down from the blush-inducing blue eyes that had stopped Brace in his steps on a rooftop elsewhere in Spiral. "You might guess, Savin, that I have a rather special interest in your doings."

The Patron fell to his knees and sobbed, burying his face in his palms as he bent over fully and pressed his forehead to the ground.

Anastasia rolled her eyes. "I give up."

"I've had a rather special interest in you myself, if you are truly the goddess Anastasia and not some prankster spirit. Do you like this piece? It's called, 'The Truth of the Muse.' I think it says something, don't you?"

Anastasia stepped toward the painting and studied it, moving her eyes over every inch, and over the carved bone-white frame that held it. "The blood is real, but those are animal bones, Savin. You're overcharging your simple friend."

"Do you take no offense?" He said, pressing closer. "Is this not truth?"

"You're very bold presuming to speak to me that way when I hold you in such obvious contempt. Mind your words. My temper is close to the surface right now."

Philosopher's words still rung fresh in her ears, and the horror of his actions was still settling in. The thought of her fellow Amaranthines trapped in their own den worlds and possibly just as compromised made her seethe under every pore of her skin. This circled a heart freshly broken at the totality with which Philosopher had abandoned and betrayed her.

She had wandered the streets sobbing, throwing mobs aside with a pass of her hand and rendering them unconscious, but stopping just short of killing anyone.

Yet, she almost did. Time and again, she had to stay her hand from a surge of anger or sorrow that would have made her swat down those mobs like flies. She could still wipe them all out if she wanted to. It could take a bit more effort than she was used to, sure, but she was still powerful. She was still a goddess.

A goddess being held in contempt by her now ex-love and who knew how many in Spiral, all because she never intervened when they begged her to.

Or half obeyed, really. She still whispered to people and sent them onto collision courses with their destinies. She probably did that more than any other Amaranthine, and she wasn't above approaching the odd soul individually over the centuries to comfort or counsel them. Much of which, she knew, went against her people's laws, anyway.

She was lost in her own contradiction, realizing her genuine hypocrisy, and becoming sickened by it. What was the point? What was the point of any of it? If violence they wanted, violence they could probably have until they were sick of it, too. Was that how to save herself? Was that how to save her people, her world?

Her head spun with the implications until she wandered into this part of town. Under a veil of her tears she felt the presence of Savin and his Patron. Savin's gallery was hidden inside a warehouse used for grain in the past and entrance was granted by invitation only. She knew he specialized in dark arts, arts that glamorized darkness, hatred and suffering. She also knew why.

Savin seemed fearless in goading her. "It would be a dark blessing to see you act on such a grim impulse, goddess. At least you would act. More than you've done to intercede in any misfortune that's ever wound through the streets of Spiral."

"I know you're a Mindful and probably one of my most hateful critics," she told him. "I know you caught the Withering when you were young and it took your arms and wracked your body. I know those painkiller herbs barely work and that healing stone is the only thing keeping you on your feet. I know you blame me for your suffering and I know you cried my name countless times when the Withering took you. Obviously, I wasn't moved."

His eyebrows furrowed over angry eyes. "It seems I am entitled to my contempt, then. You heard it all and did nothing! Here I am now, old and spent, body inching toward a final, painful oblivion, and you stand here as careless about my suffering as you stand there in the painting. Truth of the Muse!"

"It never occurs to you people that your gods are not unfettered beings who can spill their power over into your world at a whim, does it? I've talked myself into exhaustion on the point already. No, I did not help you. I can tell you the Withering was not my creation, either.

" I'll tell you this, too. You are responsible for how you reacted to your own pain. I didn't decide that. You let it poison you and you let it make you hateful and spite driven. You always had choices. You had other roads to take through your misery, but you went out of your way to take the darkest one. How am I responsible for your decisions?"

Savin stared at her, head moving side to side like a curious bird for a moment. "You could have done something. Anything."

"Could I? That's what you think? You've decided that I had unquestionable power to change everything. You decided that, not me. You spent all of your decisions in the wrong place."

"Do you think you can second guess my entire life this late in my days, Muse? The concrete has set, dried, and cracked with age. You can't sting me with your words."

"That's not entirely my intention here. I know you can't be saved. I don't even need to look into your mind or heart for that one. How telling that you think it's all about you, as usual." She turned to the Patron. "Why are you buying this art?"

"My lady, I'm sorry, I'm so sorry, I'm not worthy…"

"Shut up and talk. Why are you with this disarming curator at all?"

Savin bristled behind her. Anastasia felt the heat of his glare on her neck and ignored him completely.

"My lady," the Patron sputtered, "It's because this makes me feel. So much of what the city releases to us is so, so...bland. It doesn't challenge the viewer. It tells no stories. This does. I want it for my own private use."

"And very probably to be the envy of the dark art underground. Tell me, do you think I'm offended by it? Should I be?"

The Patron reared up on his haunches and looked at the painting and then at the Muse. "I don't know. It says something unkind about you."

"Not anything I haven't heard lately from other sources. Between us, I'm not sure I disagree with the criticism now. As for unkind things, trust me, I think I'm old enough not to care. People have said cruel things about me since the beginnings of your world. Do you blame me for not wiping out all your troubles and cares without a flick of my wrist?"

He considered this carefully, eyes moving between the curator and the Muse several times. "As I don't know everything involved with your decision making, my lady, I can't assign blame to anyone."

The curator snarled under his breath mask. Anastasia turned back to him, eyes cold. "He's wiser than you are, Savin. For all your mind, you haven't a clue."

"He is welcome to his willful ignorance. You being real does not release you from culpability. It makes your indecision over the years thrice over damning."

"Rest assured, I'm well aware that my point of view may have been wrong all of this time. The great love of my many lifetimes just showed me that with how far he's gone to hurt the rest of my people. I may have been in error. I may need a more direct approach to undo all of this. I'll tell you this much, Savin. It won't involve hoarding art away where the world can't see it. Even dark art has its place and I will never be the one to silence it."

Anastasia held up her hand and flicked her wrist. Three large key rings packed with ring-coins appeared. She dropped them at Savin's feet. "Fifteen hundred rings. You, take the painting and go. I forbid you to hide it away. Display it with pride and tell people it's a gift to you from the Muse herself, on the occasion she stopped questioning her own direction in this world."

The Patron stared at the money on the floor with wide eyes, then scrambled to take the painting off the wall. He thanked Anastasia over and over again as he heaved it onto his back and hurried out of the chamber. Savin kept his eyes level on the Muse.

"As for you," she said, " Don't think for a second that I'll let you torch anything here. You'll find that every painting here, distasteful as many are, just became fireproof. You won't be able to break or cut them, either. They'll endure until the end of the riots at the very least. I won't stop art of any kind being made, but I will never allow its destruction out of hand."

"You would leave all of this for those raging animals?"

"You were paid what you claimed due. You had no intention of keeping these. You've lost nothing that you haven't already written off. Has it ever crossed your mind that these rioters might not be so difficult if their souls had been better fed? I'm ending the government's involvement in processing and approving art of any kind tonight. I'm freeing it. Right back into the hands of the people."

Savin's eyes wilted. Art flowing through the streets meant his collection had just devalued considerably. While this gallery was a loss in his eyes, he had other prizes secreted away that he had planned to sell hidden from the King's eyes. The forbidden art that had fueled his fortune had just lost all rarity.

"This is how you use your power, then? The moment you return, you crush my fortunes in pure spite!"

"Once again, it's all about you, isn't it? You selfish old beast. This is what's right for Spiral now. Your bitterness has failed to move me and it hasn't cowed me in the slightest. I'm glad I never spent my favor on such a twisted heart. You're against everything I've taught my muses to believe in. You're responsible for the choices you've made up to now. By all means, keep making them. Don't look to me for resolution. You could have learned a lot from the old sculptor, Pyrek."

"So, I was never wrong! You are the vain, apathetic monster I always thought you to be!"

"I was never apathetic!" she spat at him, and he recoiled from the fury that scalded her eyes. "I never approved of my kind sitting idly by and only whispering to you from hidden places. I've probably broken these precious laws of ours more often than any other Amaranthine, but because I do them here and only rarely, I'm not punished as I might deserve. No one was closer to humanity than I was, no one. Not any of my kind. If I was in the worlds ruled by my former lover, I might pay a high price for my works."

Anastasia darkened. The shadows are her deepened and her voice took on a new edge. "I came into this life covered in the blood of those who meant to harm me. I've distanced myself from that as much as I could over the centuries but for a time, I was something as horrible as my beloved Philosopher. He had to pull me out of that darkness and he never forgot it. I wasn't the gentle Muse you've known from myth and legend. For a short time I was destruction itself, on a level my old love cringed to behold. Would you have me be that thing again, Savin?"

"Would it make you something more active in the lives of those around you, I wonder? Would you be known for *doing* instead of whispering?" He stared at her over his breath mask, eyes narrow. The gliphid cowered behind him now.

"Would you have me kill and punish? The more I did, the more easy it would become. It would give me delusions of righteousness. I'd be cavalier about every punishment eventually. When would I cross the line between being a gentle Muse and a terrifying goddess? Would I even know when I did?"

"Then you are truly an irresponsible goddess, if you can't use your vast 'wisdom' and power to manage yourself. I remain unmoved: What good can you possibly be? Is it not said that evil flourishes from the inaction of the good? How are you anything but evil now for your evasion?"

Anastasia stared at him. Venom began to bubble in her heart. Long had she tried to avoid hate and negativity, but this one, this crippled old demon of a human was hitting all the raw nerves recent events had left exposed.

Savin pressed the advantage, taking two unsteady steps forward but staying upright. "Those among us who called out to you and suffered from your passive regard have no interest in hearing you excuse yourself for your indolence. Your city shakes itself apart and you wander in here, alone, indifferent to the violence wracking your streets. Who would worship you for that?"

"What would you have me do, Savin? Kill them all? Knock them out? Suppress them somehow? Exert my divine authority so they can resent me for doing that too? How long before they rebel against my word? How often do I use my power to contain them? When would I become a tyrant? Do you know how fast?"

"Fine words when the riots you caused are killing innocents

throughout the city."

Anastasia raised her hand toward Savin, and the old man backed away. She twisted her wrist and closed her fingers, and he lifted off the ground. "I could start with you, you black hearted beast. I could pluck those spindly legs right off of you like you were a bug and all of your name calling and cursing would fall on deaf ears. If I followed your 'advice.'"

"Don't try to intimidate me. You're acting on the same arrogant self-indulgence I accuse you of. For all my rancor, I am not a threat. I am the most helpless creature you've met. Striking me down makes you the tyrant you fear to become." He chuckled. "It is a short distance indeed between your worry and your fears."

Anastasia lowered her hand, and Savin dropped. His gliphid helped him stand again while she glared at him.

"Is that what I have to do to save my city? Do I have to forsake being the Goddess of Passion and become a gaoler to it instead?"

"Ask the corpses beyond these walls their opinion of you walking the streets and presumably stepping over them to get here."

"I warn you one last time, Savin. Don't assume you know better than you do about my kind. Don't assume you can hold us accountable when you have no capacity to understand what drives us. There is a proverbial big picture far beyond your scope to understand."

"Unimportant. I see the math on the blackboard as it stands regardless. You'll see the same numbers when a body count is tallied, lives lost because your wounded pride was more important than your people."

The Muse stopped and stiffened. Her eyes search for something in the air around her, then her jaw set tight.

"My temple just came under attack, Savin. I can feel it. I'm tempted to apply the weight of your criticisms there. I haven't decided what to do with you yet, so I warn you not to give me any ideas. If I do become a punisher of men, you may be the first to know."

Then, she was gone. Simply gone. In her absence, he heard that the chaos outside had drawn closer.

"Lock all the doors and windows!" Savin yelled to his gliphid. He braced himself against a pillar. "Go! Everything! We'll set every barrier we can against the rioters if they come to our doors. These are still my property!"

The gliphid bowed and vaulted off, clearing the chamber in three easy leaps.

The herb burner was left behind. It dangled from the tube that connected it to this breathing mask. He crouched, set his foot on the herb burner and pulled. His mask came undone and fell off, revealing a missing nose and missing mouth, teeth bared almost to the back of his jaw in a false grin. He felt the herbs wear off and the pain in his body returning. It was easier to hate without his mind swimming in a numbing haze.

This is not over between us, Muse. This is not over. You will hear from me again and I will reward you for your negligence. Somehow, some way, I will punish you.

> "Spiral's seeming joy is just the cork in a wine bottle. It's stopping all the turmoil underneath but in no way do we cure it. There will come a day when all of our tempers are going to flare from being subdued so long, and we'll settle accounts with our neighbors well beyond the means of gentle talking. Our tragedy is that somehow, no one else sees this coming."
>
> **- Erben Lohk, Spiral social researcher to King Ronmacharte**

The riots had spread to most of Spiral.

The mob became less about ideology and more about tearing the world apart. What had begun as angry chants and pumping fists became vicious smiles and wanton crime. The city guards were falling back to their barracks as generations of buried discontent mingled with the panic over the goddess to throw down all sense of order. No longer did the people of Spiral keep silent about inequity, as they saw it. Everything was fair game now – be it a government policy, a well-known local event, or the mere jealousy of the have nots versus the haves. Spiral learned the freedom of howling the grievances that life in the city insisted they ignore.

It didn't help that a dark god was in the shadows, fanning the flames.

Brace pulled on Anathea's arm. "Don't go that way, come on. Everything's going to Hell out here."

She glared at him. It wasn't the first time she had tried to break away. They had passed dozens of people injured in the riots. With each one, Anathea stopped and applied her healing magics the best she could. Those she couldn't save, she comforted with a different library of spells to ease their passing. The death toll citywide was skyrocketing.

"I'm a healer, Brace! This is my calling!"

It's another healer's calling. Stay out of sight as much as much as you can. Pull the cloak over your head and hide yourself, for the Muse's sake."

"But people need my help!"

"They'll be helped! You don't have the whole damned city on your shoulders!"

The fact was that Brace remembered how resentfully people had looked at her during the Nightsong. The closer they got to her Inn, the more he worried that those sentiments might become violence. If the people in Spiral were so difficult under the best of circumstances....well, he certainly saw what humanity's "perfect city" was capable of now. Maybe it always was, he thought, and all the wordplay about the good and civic minded citizen of Spiral was as realistic as the Cloud Hoppers he drew pictures of in his youth.

Anathea obeyed, but with stiff lipped protest. They had found a cloak easily enough in the castoffs around the street. They walked together for another block into the wake of the riot, where buildings burned and bodies littered the street.

Brace stayed close to her as they slowly moved through the debris. "Everyone has a grudge," he told her. "This is what the heart of Spiral is laid bare. Without law and order, we're as bad anything Thurach had to offer."

They found Gress' Inn, then. What was left of it. The mobs had put it to the torch some time ago. Only smoking wood remained. Gress, they saw, had been bludgeoned to death in the street.

Brace held his breath. There was a note pinned to Gress' body, folded over in the breeze. He straightened it.

ELF HUGGER

"Oh, no," he whispered. "We need to get out of here. Now."

He narrowly dodged a rock thrown at him from nearby. It was easily the size of his fist and it landed hard against the curb. A rioter emerged from between two buildings nearby and charged at him.

Anathea released a blast of amber energy from her palm. The rioter flew back ten feet and skidded to a stop.

More of them were emerging now. Coming out of buildings, coming around corners. Anathea counted about thirty of them. All of them armed with clubs and kitchenware.

Anathea tapped the two outermost crystals on her chest. She placed her hands together, brought all her fingers in toward her palms to cup her hands, then threw her arms wide, palms open.

An amber shield appeared around them, pouring a colored filter over the approaching crowd.

"Are you hurt, Brace?" She started doing hand and finger combinations to prepare her next spell.

"Maybe I can reason with them."

"No, you can't. You were right. We need to leave."

"Can that shield of yours move with us?"

"No, it can't."

"Then I think we have a problem."

The mob reached the shield. They surrounded it and began to beat upon it. It rippled with every blow.

"Do you have anything, like, area-of-effect?"

"Not this close, I don't. I could try to cast them to sleep but I'd have to drop the shield to put my full power behind it."

She pushed outward with her hands. Her reinforcement spell

darkened the amber tones and pushed the barrier outward another five feet.

Anathea held a hand outward to sustain the shield. The more the faux wall stopped them, the angrier the crowd got. More and more they beat against the shield.

Brace pulled the golden quill from his jacket. Knowing now that it could cut flesh as fast as any blade, he held it at the ready, prepared to stab it deep into any rioter.

"What do I do to help?" Brace cried.

"Just get ready to run."

"You're not suggesting I just leave you here?"

"I've lived ninety years. That's healthy enough a span for anyone. Longer than many humans."

"Don't give me....wait, you're what?"

She sighed. "I keep it well."

"Well, shut up. I'm not leaving you." He looked around for a weapon and picked up a broken chair leg.

"Humans. You're all so exasperating."

"Part of our charm."

Then, someone whistled. It was a loud, sharp whistle. It carried all the way down the street. Everyone looked.

Sitting on a rooftop beside them, outside of Anastasia's shield, sat Tyr, hammer across his lap. His voice filled the streets. "Might I have a word?"

Someone let fly an arrow. Tyr caught it between two fingers. "Come now! Enough of that!" He stood up and holding it by the point, he flung it back where it came from. A bowman on a rooftop across the stretch cried out, and fell off the roof to the street below.

Tyr hopped down from the roof as easily as hopping off a curb, then walked straight through Anathea's shield. He gave it a tap with his fingers. "There. That'll hold. Relax, elf."

Anathea slowly relaxed, growing more alarmed. She was straining beneath the shield before, but now it was completely self-sustaining. It had even grown harder.

"How did you do that?"

"You're going to say that a lot in the future. Hello, beautiful. I'm Tyr."

Brace shook his head and crossed his arms. He suddenly preferred the mob.

"I'm Anathea. No longer of anything. I'm a visitor to Spiral."

"We are all blessed to behold your beauty, kindly elven princess." He kissed her hand.

Brace cleared his throat. "She's not a princess. She's a healer. Just saying."

"Show me a healer without a noble soul and I'll shall you a warhammer without a handle. You're princess enough for me."

Brace caught Anathea's slight blush and felt butterflies dying in his stomach. He decided to press the immediate concern:

"Anyone got a plan for the mob? They're still sort of, you know, there."

The mob continued to pound on the shield.

"Slow, aren't they? Let me go talk to them."

Anathea pulled his arm as he turned to walk away. "They'll kill you!"

"Look, we're getting along already. Don't worry. I've got this."

Tyr marched outside the shield. The mob backed away and

stopped moving.

"Let me be brief. Your goddess fell. She is real, and she is far more human than you ever imagined. She is full of love, warmth and generosity, but she couldn't impugn your free will. All of this was designed for your self-direction. Human problems beg human solutions because relying on the gods will make you weak. You'll lose too much responsibility and with that, any sense of your own power. She never ignored you prayers. She never ignored your will. If you look at so many of your wants, you'd realize she could never fulfill them without bending other people to your will, perhaps wildly against their natures. That sits in conflict with everything the good Muse holds dear."

He took their weapons away, one by one as he spoke, and threw them to the ground. "I know you have your frustrations. Bills. Love. Hate. War. Oppression. Loneliness. Heartbreak. I sympathize. So does she. Yet she's always given you release through the greatest of her works. When was the last time you lost yourselves in a painting? When did you list sink into a book or some other story and let it take you somewhere else? Has anyone in earshot sighed at a poem in the last week? Have you marveled at a sculpture or even someone beautiful walking down the street? Not in lust, but in awe that someone like that could move through the world and leave color in their wake?"

He stood feet apart, shoulder width, and rested his hands on the hilt of his hammer. "All of this has been caused by an enemy of Anastasia the Muse. This has broken her resolve and her heart. She is as wounded and lost as any human in the same state. Do you like that thought? Anastasia, wings bent, tears spilling out of her eyes and feeling so overwhelmingly alone? With no one to talk to and no one to turn to who doesn't want something from her in return? Without anyone to confide in who isn't out to use her for their own ends or blame her for their own fortunes? Can you even calculate isolation like that? Every single one of you has at least one person to turn to. Does she? Can she turn to you?

He let the question hang in the air. Then he slammed his hammer into the concrete. He sent a shockwave out that unbalanced his audience. "*No.* Because you are all so busy destroying the city because she isn't running to your side and using her godly powers to serve your whims. She isn't responsible for your selfishness. She's the victim of it. Of course she would hide."

Anathea looked to Brace and then averted her eyes. Her own actions on being confronted by the Muse were no better. She had immediately accused Anastasia of shortcoming and negligence, and the Muse had even said she had just wanted someone to confide in. Someone as unique and alien to the view of the city as she herself.

"Some healer I turned out to be," she said quietly.

"It isn't too late to do her the favor she needs. End these riots. Go to your neighbors and tell them to lay down their grief. Quiet the streets of Spiral. Do everything you can to reverse this. Cooperate with the guards and make peace wherever you find strife. The Muse is preparing to rise again and she may yet look each of you in the eye with thanks in her own. You know now she's real. You know what I describe is far from impossible. Take the stand that counts. Save the city of the Muse. Save yourselves."

The rest of the mob began to lay down their weapons. Muttering among themselves, they parted ways. Some of them looked to Tyr and nodded.

Tyr touched the shield with his finger. It popped out of existence.

"That does it for this street. I think I know what would help, too. You're a healer, yes? Heal as many as you can. This guy can help, too. Bandage and tend. Tell them stories, soothe their minds. More importantly, let everyone see you healing the wounded, openly."

Anathea arched an eyebrow when she looked at Brace. He cleared his throat and looked at Tyr.

"Well, you saved our lives. That's entirely good, yes. But how did you find us? How did you know we were in trouble?" Brace stood next to Anathea and crossed his arms.

"I could sense the elf-magic. She's glassed. That's a rare thing. Only elves have mastered it, and it puts off a pretty impressive signature. Couldn't miss it." He nodded to Anathea. "Healing, yes?"

"Healing. It's my calling. I can do it."

"Do it," Tyr nodded. "As much as you can. Let them see you healing, too. Their friends, neighbors and family, all of them. Don't hide it at all. I'm going to go drop that speech on a few more blocks. We can reverse the course but it'll take time. I can count on you too, right?"

"My name is Brace, and yes."

Tyr smiled and tapped the side of his head with a wink. "I know where you got that quill, Brace. The original owner has been a friend of mine for time out of mind. I know that means she feels you can be trusted as a friend. Remember as much of my speech just now as you can. Go deliver as many of those words as you're able to across the streets. Put it in your own words if need be. You have a fine tool for it. Just get the word out. Call it out on street corners and write them on walls. The two of you can move mountains here. I'll see where else I can go for the same."

He turned without another word, hefted the hammer over his shoulder, and walked partway down the street before someone from a rooftop threw a large rock at him. He swung his hammer and hit it back. It sped out of sight and someone across the way grunted "ACK!" and fell off the roof.

"I said stop it!" he shouted.

"The muses wander Spiral and inspire everyone they can. Art is their love but they do their best to comfort and encourage everyone. They are trusted counselors, friends, lovers for a night or a lifetime, but I assure you, one thing they are not is weak. The muses are trained in how to defend themselves to the best of their ability and I promise you, they have had very good trainers. Let no one doubt that these young men and women are capable fighters."

- **Matron Violetta, predecessor of Matron Cor**

Matron Cor had run the temple for twenty-two years. Long enough for her frame to bear the weight of age and for her ink black hair to shoot through with gray. Whereas she was once the most beautiful of the temple muses in her youth, her wide blue eyes and dimpled smile having inspired some of the best artwork in her generation (stuck in the city vaults yet as it was), she now stood as the essence of beautiful motherhood. She was aging as gracefully as she knew how but she did not let the extra pounds on her frame or the marks around her eyes to slow her passion for the message of the Muse.

Her once revealing silks had long since given way to swirling white dresses, golden cords entwined around her stomach holding it all in place. Her warm and playful eye still inspired her fellow muses onward in their doings, even if her relationship with them was less in youthful spirit and more than knowing guardian.

Tonight her eyes were strained with worry. The temple muses had barricaded the entrance to the temple and a cordon of guards maintained them outside. Most of the rioters were bypassing the temple. After all, if the Muse was real, attacking her chosen children wasn't the best idea.

Still, small mobs still attacked. Gangs, really. They would

scream for the Muse to show herself and demanded their prayers be answered, or they howled their ambitions for specific muses in the temple. This particular crowd was growing in size. Quickly.

What they did not suspect, these potential attackers, was that the muses were often trained very well in self-defense. It had proven more than once to be critical in private one on one musing sessions with clients less noble than their declared intentions. The muses stood ready in the main hall wearing practical, brown leather armor against white flowing garments. They held short swords and steel bucklers ready. Their hair was swept back and pinned into place.

Each one was ready to kill to protect the temple.

Matron Cor walked among them wielding only a long, gilded staff. Gems of amber and red were set in both ends.

A large mob was crashing against the guards. This was the largest mob yet, easily two hundred people deep. They had only thirty guards around the temple who were tired and tapped of their magics, positioned closest to the many entrances of the grand hall. There were no doors to lock. The grand hall was expected to be open to everyone, day or night. No barrier saved them but the failing guards. This time, Matron Cor expected her muses to fight.

She saw the guards giving in. Obeying their vehement wishes, the small army of muses did not interfere. Disobeying their vehement wishes, the muses did not flee.

"Stand fast!" she shouted to them. "Strike true and do not hesitate."

The muses took position to meet the rush and leaned forward, shields front and swords pointing toward the coming breach.

The air changed when the mob surged in. The yells outside now violated the temple walls, the acoustics designed to accentuate sound now broadcasting war. It was a mob covered in ashes and blood, waving makeshift weapons and screaming.

The muses ran forward. Throats practiced at singing shouted as one. They crashed into the crowd with their shields and began slashing with their swords. The second breach opened nearby, and another wave of the muses charged. Five of them remained with Matron Cor.

Blood ran on both sides. The muses were holding their ground, winning the fight at first. A collection of rioters' bodies lined the perfect tile. Blood eclipsed the portraits of Anastasia cobbled into the floor.

A third breach opened behind them. The great hall was soon to be flooded with raging citizens.

Matron Cor charged. She spun her staff backward and forward. The red gems flared, fireballs erupting from her staff wherever it contacted a rioter, burning them as it knocked them aside. When she spun the staff to deflect attacks, the defensive gems kicked and bursts of amber sheltered her. Any who thought the older woman would be easy prey died ignorant of her two decades of fighting skill.

The mob broke against the first two defensive lines. They retreated covered in fresh scarlet. Half of the muses from these two positions ran back toward Matron Cor. The third mob was pouring through in greater numbers, however. Muses fell here and there and they pressed inward.

As they crested the chamber, the wave of rioters fanned out, smashing sculptures and statues. They torched paintings and muses alike. Matron Cor and her survivors fell back towards the base of the statue, losing ground by the moment.

This is it, Matron Cor thought. Her heart broke for every muse motionless on the floor. *This is it. I've failed the temple. I've failed the Muse herself.*

Anastasia walked up behind her. "Relax. You're doing fine."

She motioned with one hand and every rioter in the temple fell through the floor and disappeared. She touched a finger to her forehead and turned in a circle, sensing each muse that could be saved and healing them. The dead, no one could help.

Matron Cor and the muses faced Anastasia in her human form, then went down on both knees and averted their eyes. They placed their palms on the ground.

"Kneel, then. It may appropriate." Anastasia watched them take a knee but her heart ache. Tears threatened her eyes. If she was to rule them now, was this truly how it was meant to be? Would her friends become grovellers?

Anastasia went from muse to muse, helping the previously wounded stand up. She placed discarded shields over the faces of the fallen. "I didn't feel this happening immediately. I'm sorry for my...distraction."

"Surely you don't mean to apologize to us, my lady. You're our goddess." Matron Cor helped herself up with her staff. The younger muses gathered to her.

"I've found that gods owe apologies more frequently than I ever expected. I'm keeping faith with that. I'm not perfect. I'm not even sure who I am, now."

The muses were together now at the feet of her statue. Each looked to her with adoration and hope.

There wasn't a look if anger or disappointment amongst any of them, even with their dead on the floors around the hall. Here was the one place where she felt unquestioned. Already it felt alien to stand there as herself, beyond reproach. It took her several moments to recover from the shock of not being berated, and briefly she wondered if there was something wrong with all of *them*.

No, of course not. They were loyal and they believed. They looked to her with love in their eyes, ready to follow her every word.

She trembled for a moment, wondering how far that would take them if left to their own devices, and saw the long-held fear of the Amaranthines flicker before her mind's eye.

Still, they had lived with the idea that she was real their entire lives. Skeptics and cynics might have their place throughout Spiral, but here she was the goddess, the Muse. They believed in her and welcomed her with the most open hearts she'd felt outside of Pyrek the Old or her dear friend, Tyr.

She needed to believe in them too, she realized. She took a steady breath and calmed herself. Than she began to speak.

"I've been brought low by an enemy I never knew I had. He's known in some places as the 'Lord of Ten Shadows.' He is no friend to us. He has engineered this nightmare around us to humble me. He seeks to rule over me and take me from this world forever. He has done a very effective job of wounding me deeply."

Her fingers brushed against the cooling face of a golden haired muse of perhaps sixteen. She had died from a massive wound to her throat. Anastasia summoned the blood away from her and let it drop on a dead rioter. Now clean, she arranged the body neatly and put a shield over her face.

"I have a better idea now how to fight for Spiral. I can't meet him on his terms, but I can undercut his influence. He's inflamed the darker aspects of the human soul in the city. Those prone to anger or misgiving are finding themselves impossible to control. He is not giving them anything that isn't already there. He's escalating it instead. He could do nothing else without betraying his point about free will."

"We stand with you," Matron Cor declared. The muses nodded vigorously and cheered.

Anastasia smiled. "I know. And I love you all for that. I love those that fell here. I'll never take my world for granted again, I promise you. I'm going to rule openly from now on. I'll guide everyone the best I can. I won't be a rumor or an opinion or a what if. I'll labor to bring peace to this city and to every soul here. Problem is, the Lord of Ten Shadows has robbed me of most of my power. I need you all to act for me. Would you?"

The muses cheered and surrounded her, hugging her and reassuring her. "Tell us what to do. We're yours. We won't let you down." This she heard over and over.

"Matron Cor is going to be my second in command. Obey her as unconditionally as ever but now, know that her word comes from me. Cor, pick some muses and send them to the King. They will ask him politely to throw open the art vaults. You know the art horde they're keeping down there.

" I want the vault doors taken off the hinges and destroyed. I want the guards sent away. Tell him this comes from me directly. He's already met me in person, he and his wizard, Cappus. Warn him that if I have to come and deal with this in person, neither of them will stand higher than a roach tomorrow morning."

Cor pointed at four muses, named them, and nodded. The muses bowed and rushed to their duty. Anastasia motioned for Matron Cor to stay. "I'm not risking you out in the open yet. We're going to do something bold."

"What has your mind, my lady?"

"First off, gorgeous work with that staff. Bravo. I am most impressed! Second, gather the surviving guards outside and tell them to find wagons. Large wagons. Use them to gather the art we're about to free. All of it. Songs, sculptures, paintings, drawings, books plays, anything. Everything. Get them all. You're going to take them to every corner of the city. Don't worry, there are decades of art down there in the vaults, more than enough for our purposes. Tell the guards to take them everywhere. But you stay here with me."

Matron Cor bowed and went outside to deliver Anastasia's

orders. The guards were searching the grounds for the vanished rioters.

Anastasia paced around her statue, waiting for time to pass. Patience wasn't necessarily her virtue and stress only made the waiting worse.

Talking to Pyrek, Tyr and even Savin, she had realized how her own vulnerability was failing her people. Spiral needed less her self-pity and more her intervention. Curse her distraction! Philosopher had a talent, however; he always knew how to destabilize his prey. Breaking their straight lines of thought was a specialty of his.

The best way to do that, she realized, was to charge headlong into Philosopher's trap. Since she had fallen, she had tried to remain unseen. This uncertainty had fanned the problem, not erased it: Undoubtedly Philosopher's plan.

However, Philosopher apparently gambled that her want to stay invisible would guide her responses to this damnable act of his. She had a new idea now: She would undo Philosopher's paradox from the inside. She would strive to be seen. She would make some changes around here. She would visibly lead. Once this was all done with, Spiral could enter a new age.

Best of all, she didn't need the full measure of her powers to do it. She needed to give a damn.

Matron Cor came inside and said, "My lady, the guards are curious, what came of the rioters? There were so many."

Anastasia darkened. "I transported them all a several miles above Spiral. I meant for them to see their deaths coming for several minutes so they could think about what happened to them and why. They should start hitting the streets any moment now."

The muses gasped. Some applauded.

One of them, a girl of fifteen with pale skin and dark red hair, whimpered and hung her head. She must have been new to the temple, as Anastasia had no memory of her before recent events. But she had donned the silk, leather and armor of a muse and she had fought among their number without hesitation. Of all the muses present and their varied reaction, she felt the heartbreak in the girl penetrating her own spirit.

Anastasia approached her. "What's wrong? They attacked the temple. They killed these muses in front of you."

"This can't be right, my lady. Did they really mean to kill us all?"

"Most intended to. I should know. Look what they've done!"

"But they couldn't stand a chance against you. How can they learn they were wrong now? How can they improve?"

Anastasia's finger twitched. She could sense the falling rioters slowing in the sky.

"Give me your word on the matter, then," she told the girl. "Tell me why I should let them live. I'm a goddess and I have to assert myself now. I've been torn down for *not* taking measures like this at every turn. You could ask a certain curator named Savin Durs about that. Perhaps if I was quicker, fewer of your sisters would be dead. How is this not my fault? How are the dead all around Spiral not my failure?"

"My lady, please. This can't be who you are. This is against everything I was taught about you. This is against everything I loved about you."

"Those soft old legends? Do you think I've never taken lives before?"

"I think you're strong enough not to. I want to believe you are. I want you to believe you are, too. Please, my lady, please. Spare them. Give them a chance to learn. If they're still foul things after the fact, I'll say nothing for any punishment you wish on them. But please, please, give them a chance to be something else. We're creators. We can't be lead by a mass murderer."

The Muse frowned. Moisture gathered in the corner of her eyes. "Mass murderer. Me, a mass murderer. Failed goddess or mass murderer. No way to win."

"Whatever you would be, you would not Anastasia the Muse anymore. That's not worth throwing away on them. Don't we matter? Do the values you've taught us about love, truth and beauty mean anything if you slaughter the people we need to reach most?"

The girl knelt and hung her head then. "Forgive my contradicting you, my lady. I just...had a different view of who you are. Of course, I can't see the things that you can see."

Anastasia was silent for a minute, holding her face in her hands. Her shoulders trembled. Then she drew her hands back and composed herself.

"What is your name?" The Muse asked.

"I'm Petrenella. Daughter of the King of Spiral."

The other muses gasped. Matron Cor drew close and checked her from head to toe for wounds, her eyes wide. "A Princess of Spiral here, in a battle zone! You told me your name was Leigh!"

"I told you the name I choose. I'm Leigh Veeh now. If anyone asks, I'm from the Vomacka district. I've chosen the life I want. I want to be a muse, like all of you. I am Leigh." She looked at Anastasia. "As long as my goddess remains one that I can follow."

Anastasia smiled, but it was a bitter smile. She ran a hand through Leigh's hair. "You wonderful, wonderful girl. I'll give you what you want. I'll spare them. Not without punishment of some kind, though. I will compel them to leave Spiral and never to return. They will never know comfort or love again on their own terms and if seen in my city they will be imprisoned at the very least. If they can reforge themselves into something new from that, I'll forgive them. This is my offer for their lives."

Leigh knelt, arms out to her sides and palms upward. "I thank you, my goddess. I promise I'll be a good muse. You won't regret this."

"'No power of creation can condone destruction.' That's what my old friend Sera'loq would say if he was here. I think he'd really like you, Leigh." Leigh smiled and looked away, blushing. Anastasia felt the warmth in her heart, and a burst of humble respect. "Incidentally, Leigh, I see you've been having trouble with your father about becoming a muse. Don't worry about it. You're with us now. I think I'd rather keep you here for a while as is, so pardon me for sending other people to secure the art from the palace. Less drama that way. I'd rather you made yourself at home here."

Leigh nodded, dimming. "I'm not ready to see my father again just yet. Maybe not for a while. I'd like to go see the gardens, if you would allow it. I've always loved gardening. Also, can I have a fuzzymug? I love animals most of all."

"So, life itself is your art, Leigh?"

Anastasia made a mental note to have Leigh trained as the next Matron of the temple.

> "The riots ground to a halt. The guards asserted themselves in the city again. Exhaustion reached every citizen if the violence hadn't. The death toll was in the hundreds and the damage blackened the city like nothing since Thurach. Rising from the ashes of this discontent came the goddess herself, swearing better times for us all. Time would tell if this was a promise kept."
>
> - Storyteller Simone Decomule, Spiral oral historian

It took the rest of the night, but the wagons of art were circulated around Spiral. Rioters were told they could take one piece of art for every weapon or torch they turned over to the city guardsmen. Meanwhile, Tyr's oratory was swaying the people blocks at a time. Even Brace made his share of impassioned speeches, using his gift for words to contain Tyr's intent. Anathea healed dozens per street. Where she was shunned before, she was now offered food and water and comfort. Soon she had a team of nurses and magical healers following her lead, and she commanded them to their tasks with great competence.

The riots stopped by the afternoon of the next day. The people were too tired for violence and yet too tired to repair.

There was a great audio system built throughout Spiral that was powered by magic. It was called the Piping, and this is how the music of the Nightsong reached the people of Spiral every night. From high above the city in the temple tower, muses given to song and their gliphid companions drummed out the evening rites, their magic carrying their music across the streets.

Now, Anastasia and her friends stood in the tower together, gathered on the main stage. The usual musical instruments were pushed against the wall. Anastasia held a golden necklace with a glowing purple gem up to her neck and fastened it down so the jewel hung loose against her throat. She tapped it to activate it, and her voice flowed through Spiral.

"I am Anastasia the Muse. I'm sorry I'm not perfect, but if it's any consolation, I was never intended to be. I'm part of a race called the Amaranthines, a race that's stood in ruin for centuries. I had a purpose among my people, and that was the passion of mortal and immortal alike. I was to cultivate love, beauty, honesty, adventure, exploration, freedom and companionship in all of its forms, the better to remind my peers of the humanity they lost when ascending."

"All Amaranthines hold free will to be the most important quality in the universe, along with the flow of nature itself. We can't intervene in good conscience on events you set in emotion yourselves. I'm sorry if it seems I've turned a deaf ear to suffering in your families and friends and all the bad luck that's come, but by our own laws, I was forbidden to intervene. I did everything I could to make life beautiful for you all in Spiral, and elsewhere in the world, but I largely left self-determination alone. It was the only way to keep you as beautiful as you really are.

"My enemy has cast me down and taken my invisibility from you. For days I wondered how I could possibly act without making things worse. Now I believe the only way forward is through the mouth of the beast. I will go against my instinct and my nature, even some of our laws, to stand among you as one of your own and counsel you with my own hand. I will not bring you wealth, love, passion or success. You'll bring that to yourselves. But I will encourage you, and I will applaud amongst your loved ones when you achieve them. I may burst with pride over every one of you.

"There is one exception. Crimes were committed during the riots. Lives were lost and property was destroyed. I assure you I can ascertain guilt with but a glance, and specific crimes in the same look. The guilty must leave Spiral and my sight forever. Any of you that fall under my eyes with this guilt will be punished. King Ronmacharte still rules and he will rule with my word. He will uphold laws, administration, judiciary process and punishments. I will take the culture and the arts. Give him your mind, but give me your hearts.

"This could be an uncertain process and there will be need to grow and adapt on both sides, but I think we can do this painless if we all remember the good things in our lives and count our blessings. I am here with you now to count them with you. I've never done this before so openly, so I'll need your help to succeed. We can all teach other. That will be the enlightenment of Spiral.

"I will reside in the temple and the muses will be my representatives to you all. Continue to respect them and do well by them. You need not listen to a muse, but do not harm them. They are my angels and I am quick to anger where their safety is concerned.

"Tomorrow night, we will return to the tradition of the Nightsong. We've gone too long without that rite. Rest well, for I want dancing and singing like we've never before seen in the streets of Spiral. Rejoice, all. We will be one, and I love you all."

Anastasia ended the connection. Uncertainty clung to her yet, but it was time for confidence, even if it was false confidence. She turned to her oldest friend.

Tyr bowed to the Muse. She kissed his forehead. "Thank you so much. I'll never be without need of you, Tyr. Know that forever."

"Remembered well and ever." He returned to his ready position, hands on the hilt of his downturned hammer, and was otherwise quiet. He turned an eye to Brace nearby. Brace was staring after Anathea or lowering his eyes while shifting from foot to foot. Tyr looked to Anastasia and she gave him a curt nod.

Tyr took Brace by the arm. "We are going to talk later. Private business."

Brace gulped but nodded.

Anastasia's eyes lingered on him a moment before she turned to Anathea. "Anathea. I know you've found what I left you. I'm glad you got your hands on it but I was hoping I could give it to you myself. I whispered in Brace's ear to take you to the Hanging Library when he was unconscious in case I wasn't able to get back to it soon."

Anathea tensed. "I have it, yes. I've kept it safe. I just don't know what it is."

"That's the point of a good surprise, though I know that surprises aren't your favorite thing. Believe me, I mean it as a gift. I want things to be good between us as people."

"Me? I deserve no gifts. I'm happy to be alive with all we saw."

"Since I've ordered that crafted, you've saved the lives of hundreds of men, women and children in Spiral. I meant it as a peace offering before, but now it's twice that and a gift. I need to see you rewarded."

Anathea drew it out of her pouch and held it in the palm of her hand. "In spite of myself, I'm very curious what a goddess would leave me."

"It isn't arrogant to open a gift. Just break it when you're alone. It's meant only for you."

"Even though when we met, I was less than genial to you?"

"Yes. Don't sweat it."

Anathea smiled and nodded, turning the gem over and over in her hand.

Then the world shuddered and darkened, and *he* appeared, floating off center from the room and facing Anastasia. He hovered in the air, wings spread wide as his shadow blackened everything.

"Anastasia. Do you think our business finished?"

Tyr ran in front of her, hammer ready. "Michael. Don't do this. This isn't you. Please, stand down."

"Tyr. So, this is where you've been Sleeping. I am Philosopher now. I am no more Michael than you are."

Philosopher flicked a finger and Tyr flew had into a far pillar, cracking it. Anathea rushed to heal him.

"Stop it!" Anastasia shouted. "No more violence in my world! Not from you!"

"You've poisoned your own well. You know this, don't you? You have made entirely the wrong choice. Now, everything falls. Your every step will be failure. In their minds, you will always make the wrong decision. You will be hated inside a generation and wars will be fought over interpreting you. You'll find them twisting every word you speak to serve themselves and make things worse."

"I'll stand by my people, Philosopher. I won't stand with you. You and your obsolete, unproven war against an invisible fiend we can no longer confirm even still exists! You've become every bit the Great Enemy he was. How are your methods any different than his? What have you done to account for yourself?"

She marched toward him fearlessly, still in her humanized form. She pointed at him from below, a small human frame against a shadowy nightmare. "You've forsaken everything that was meant to keep you sane. I was meant to give you the human touch, and I did it time and again when you threatened to slip into this. You didn't need to be this thing to fight your Great Enemy. You did it out of fear. That's the truth of it! You were afraid you were failing at some grandiose goal that only you cared to see anymore and you went mad with your imagined responsibility. Now that we've all farmed out our own worlds it's all you can do to stay relevant among your own people! This isn't some grand stratagem to get us on the same page for some ancient duty. You're throwing a reality wide tantrum because no one's listening to you anymore!"

Philosopher lowered himself to the floor and pulled his wings in. *"Me? The Great Enemy?"*

"The Great Enemy himself. Can't find his deeds? Get a mirror!. Then we're sure to party up against him in your name. Right? You're blind to how dark and terrible you've really become. You don't have what it takes to lead us in this state. We followed you as Michael when you showed the most compassion, wisdom and love. You actually thought abandoning it was going to do you a *favor?* You thought trading all of that out for ruthlessness and sadism was an *enhancement?"*

She glared up at him, and being human-framed did little to quell her ferocity. "Do you remember when you saved me from those men? My horrible master and his disgusting friends? You took love and compassion on a mere mortal you knew nothing about. You couldn't tell what I was going to do or what I was going to be like with Amaranthine power. Yet you took this broken, delusional girl who had already been on the mad end of sanity and you made her a *goddess.* In your present state you not only would have overlooked me, you probably would have wiped me out with the entire countryside for some imagined sin or other. I would never have been known.

"Think about that. All of the love and comfort I ever visited upon you, that you always wept so to experience, all of that would never have existed. The role I played with the other Amaranthines, that would never have happened. Our people would have fallen into decadence and self-loathing and darkness untold eons ago if your compassion hadn't been reflected and amplified through me. You inspired me, and I gave that to them. I could make them remember love and passion with a caress. In this form, I was able to make you something like Michael again when you let me. All of that would have been drummed out of the world without a thought by *Philosopher.*

"That disqualifies you from judging me and my methods and my entire world. I'm employing virtues you've completely forsaken. In this form, you don't even understand them! You drove then out of yourself willingly for a garbage cause. You yourself once said 'there can be no justice without empathy.' I reject you, your idiot 'object lesson' and whatever you thought to force upon me here on the grounds that you lack any compassion to understand the consequences of your own acts. Without me to temper you, you are as lost and dark as the Great Enemy. It's only just you should follow in his footsteps as his heir."

The chamber hung quiet. Tyr watched, panting, cradled in Anathea's arms as she healed him.

Philosopher was silent for almost two minutes. Then he reached out to gently caress Anastasia's cheek, but she slapped his hand away.

"Don't even think about it. My touch is lost to you. Vanish into whatever black void your heart calls home and leave me to my people. What the Hell did you want from me? It's not like I'm a warrior, anyway."

"I could crack this world open with a sigh."

"Yes. You could. It wouldn't change one moment of truth I just dropped on you. It would prove you the equal of that which you despise. Logic your way out of that."

He paused again, then turned away, becoming indistinct. *"You may regret this one day, Anastasia. You may have set in motion events you can't turn back."*

"There will be love and laughter for every day until then. That's how you make life into art, Philosopher. Not by fearing the darkness, but living passionately in spite of it. I hope one day you regret losing your beloved Anastasia the Muse."

Philosopher's eyes turned toward Brace. Brace stepped back with a gulp but put on his bravest face. His blue eyes looked to the golden quill hidden in Brace's clothes.

The shadowy Amaranthine then turned on one foot as if to leave and faded out of existence. The room immediately returned to normal lighting.

Brace relaxed and mopped a bead of sweat off his forehead. "Was that him? That was the ex?"

"We all have an ex we'd love to forget," she said. She shifted her position in the room to Tyr with a single thought. She knelt down and held a hand out. "My friend, you didn't have to have to do that."

"Oh, shuddup. Of course I did."

"Healed?"

"Fully. Your elf is quite an expert."

"I think you should consider opening your own practice here, Anathea. Or I could easily give you your own hospital if you choose to stay."

"My own hospital?" The normally stoic elf blushed, then smiled widely. "That would be...I don't know. Brace, a word?"

"Spectacular? Amazing? Brilliant?"

"Phenomenal!"

He shook his head and said to a muse, "Why did she even ask?"

"We have a lot of work to do to restore Spiral. I'm glad you're all here with me for this. I think I'll keep this human form for a while, too. A reminder to myself about everything that's just happened. I don't want to return to the form Philosopher beloved once upon a time. Not just yet."

The Muse walked to the open wall of the tower, which overlooked the city. The sunrise was cresting the mountains behind a quilt of rainclouds. Would it rain or no? Too early to say, but there was moisture in the wind. She saw the shimmerflies landing on the rooftops of Spiral to enter their deep sleep. Gliphids would scoop them up soon to store for the renewed Nightsong.

Anastasia considered these soon-to-be-trapped shimmerflies and sighed heavily. "I hope I know what I'm doing."

> "I've always enjoyed a deep, passionate love to dash myself against."
>
> - Actress Shaelin Monmarte

Brace found Tyr the next morning in the Golden Lofts. The Lofts were a luxury hotel in one of the richer districts, and it took Brace most of his morning to get there.

The building was five stories up and made of shining marble, which captured enough sunlight to glow during the day and held enough of it after dark to glow a pale blue. The interior was a labyrinth of polished woods, and included fine wood sculptures and three dimensional murals from throughout Spiral's districts.

Everyone working there knew where Tyr was, it turned out, and they all pointed to the penthouse at the top. Brace climbed flight after flight of the winding staircase to reach him, marvelling at the waterfall that fell straight through the center of the circling staircase.

The double doors to the penthouse suite were ajar with a note on the rightmost door saying, "COME IN, BRACE. HAVE SOME BOOZE." Brace plucked it down and entered the penthouse suite quietly. He heard feminine voices beyond and saw three women getting dressed in the middle of the room.

He averted his eyes but they chided him. "Relax, sweetie," one of them said, "We're done here. Your friend is in the other room. Thank him again for us."

"Thank him for what?" Brace asked, and they giggled as they swept past him and shut the door behind them.

"Brace!" he heard Tyr shout. Even in one word he sounded well beyond drunk.

"I'm here." Brace brushed aside the door to the bedroom with his shoulder.

Tyr was lying naked in bed with a zebra bedsheet only barely covering his loins. He was muscled like a god but as drunk as a man. His hair was disheveled and his clothes were spread around the room. His metal gauntlet was lying beside the round waterbed he was sprawled upon.

"Did I come at a bad time?" Brace asked. "I could come back later."

"Nonsense! We're brothers. Come in. Have some of the draught on the table there. There's more than enough for you."

"I didn't think this could affect you anymore now that you were, you know, awakened or what have you." Brace poured himself a modest glass and sipped it.

"It affects me when I allow it to. It so happens I'm in need of libation."

"And those women that just left?"

"That was the last of them."

"Last of them?"

"There were twice as many here before. I'm afraid my appetites lean toward the insatiable."

Tyr laughed and rolled over on his bed, letting loose a burp. Brace saw blue angel wings tattooed across his back.

"I was told you wanted to see me," Brace said, voice awkward. He took another sip of the mug and tried to hide his embarrassment behind it.

"Ah, yes. Words on Anathea. That was the point."

Brace stiffened. "I'm sure there's nothing there to discuss."

"Of course there is! Of course! I'm a god, I see these things. Well, I'm a half asleep god and well inebriated, but I saw it when I was a little less muggy. Sit down, sit down."

Tyr patted the bed, but Brace's feet stayed rooted.

"I'm okay," Brace said. "I don't plan to stay long."

"Suit yourself. But talk we will. Anathea."

"What of her?"

"Why have you been such a complete ass to her?"

Brace's jaw dropped open. "I have not been an ass to her!"

"You've been clingy. You were a little too territorial about her doing the riots."

"I was protecting her!"

Tyr arched an eyebrow.

Brace blushed and hung his head.

"I'm not here to draw wounds on you, Brace. I'm just telling you this. If the spark didn't happen, the spark didn't happen. Sorry for that. You know the Muse doesn't steer people into each other like that. She can't make Anathea yours. Anathea calls the shots. A gentleman should respect that."

"Am I not a gentleman, now?"

"I don't know, aren't you? It seems you've projected some expectations on Anathea that aren't entirely fair."

Brace set down his drink and walked toward the door. Tyr flicked his finger and the doors slammed shut, hard. Brace jumped back.

"Sorry," Tyr said sheepishly. "Getting the hang of that bit. The beer's making it a little off."

"Look, I'd rather not talk about this," protested Brace. "This is all personal business."

"Anathea has saved countless people now. She did an amazing job during the riots. We owe her for that."

"Are you sure it isn't your own interest in her talking?" The jealousy in Brace's voice dripped from his lips.

"Listen to yourself. So territorial, so threatened. I flirt with everyone, okay? I've even done it to men, if that should shock you." Tyr rubbed his temples and grunted. "Besides, everyone knows my fixation and it isn't your elf."

"Anastasia."

"See? I said everyone knew." Tyr stood and held his arms out. The blanket shot around his shoulder and body and reformed into a long robe.

"Okay, that was awesome," Brace said. "But Anastasia is your 'fixation?'"

"You just conjured up her name with zero real clues on the matter, so yeah, you and the rest of Spiral must already know that. Not that it's ever been a secret. I've coveted that woman for two thousand years."

That statement hung between them in silence for a few moments.

Tyr continued on. "I have never seen anyone as beautiful as Anastasia. No one. Not ever. Not in form, not in voice, not in poise or purpose. I've never seen a more passionate, loving soul. She burns with life while others merely flicker with it. Every day is a chance to dance for her. Every day is an opportunity to sing, paint, write, perform, anything. She never tires of it, and she works so hard to draw others into that joy. I swear to you, she has the most beautiful soul in all of creation. She has a genuinely good and loving heart, whatever the wretched Mindful want to say about her."

"You've never told her any of this?"

"She's the Muse. She knows. She reads people so very, very well. This includes gods." Tyr poured himself another mug, then walked away with the pitcher and downed it in a long train of gulps. "That mug's for you if you want more," he said.

Brace took up his first mug and sipped it again. "I feel that way about Anathea."

Tyr turned to face him and pointed at him with the pitcher. "No, Brace. You think you do. You're attracted to her but I dare say you have no love for her yet. You're still glued to that moment you danced the Nightsong together. Did it ever occur to you that what she wanted was just a friend in Spiral? That woman has human men ravening after her constantly. Has it occurred to you that she's lonely? All that charm and charisma and she's so deeply lonely. You'd find a lot of people you think of as beautiful are really deeply lonely people. The treasure you gave her that night was to be an understanding hand in what had turned out to be an alienating world. She was thankful to have someone she hoped could be a good friend."

Brace digested this slowly and took several more sips from his mug in silence. Then he asked, "Is that how you connect with Anastasia?"

"Yes. In spite of my passion for her, yes. You know what treasure is that I have here, Brace?" Trust. Of all the people born in the universe, in any reality, I am one she calls brother and friend. I am a confidant she can have faith in. I was the one she came to in her darkest hour and she awakened me in this mortal flesh to help her when she needed it most. Yes, I love her beyond words. No single human woman, no half dozen, no hundred and no million of them can be Anastasia the Muse to me. Yet I know what a treasure her company is and I guard that trust with every fiber of my being."

"But you covet her, don't you? Like I do Anathea!"

"No man can help but covet her, and let her dance through the steamiest of his daydreams. But one man can stand shoulder to shoulder with her as her friend when she needs it most. I'm that trusted one. That is a luxury, Brace. Ask yourself this, do you want

Anathea for selfless reasons or selfish ones? Do you know the difference?"

Brace opened his mouth to protest, but stopped. He struggled with an argument that refused to form on the tip of his tongue, looking side to side and appearing to ready himself for a response when he'd stop and recoil.

"You built a world around her that wasn't necessarily rational. You imagined what things were going to be like with you two and you all but scripted it like a play. The moment she deviated from that you felt you lost a level of control you didn't actually have over your situation. It didn't occur to you that she might not be what you projected. You made no allowance for her to just be there on her own terms, rather than serving your fantasies."

"You're being a bit harsh, aren't you?"

"You think I say this because I can't relate?"

Brace finished the rest of his drink and put the mug down. Tyr eyed the mug he had poured earlier and said, "Are you going to drink that?"

Brace shook his head. Tyr shrugged and scooped up the mug.

"So tell me then, Tyr, what wisdom is there to be found between two men who can't have the women they want?"

"Don't be so bitter. I'm telling you the entire point. There's wisdom enough to be found here and I'm giving it to you. If you truly care about Anathea, being her friend is a grand reward. You have to do it from the right perspective though."

"What is that?"

"Don't expect it to go anywhere else. Ever. Don't do it thinking you'll be next in line or that she'll owe you romance later. Put that out of your mind. Be there because being there is the right thing to do, and she trusts you to be her friend. Separate the notion that you could or should have her on your own terms. That should be enough. If you actually care about her, that should be fine. Anything else is you gratifying yourself at her expense. That'll be obvious and she'll respond to it in kind."

Brace deflated. His shoulders slumped and he chewed on the inside of his cheeks. Tyr's hand fell heavy on his shoulder.

"Chin up, lad. I know better than anyone what it is to pine for the unattainable. I'm just giving you the best answer I've found in two millennia of craving someone like that."

"It's never hard for you to accept that? Really? Ever?"

Tyr withdrew his hand and took a deep breath, and downed half the mug in one shot.

"Brace, that woman has brought out the best in me from the beginning. All she has to do is talk to me across a counter in a cafe and she brings out the sleeping god I'd long since forsaken. She powers me to move mountains for her and pull down the stars as a gift in her honor, and I could sing ballads a thousand years in gratitude for her making me remember what's really vital in life. That's enough for my loyalty ever forth."

"What if she turns away from you one day? What then?"

"Then I better live up to what she taught me. Though I imagine I'd go through metric tons of beer."

Tyr finished the rest of his mug. "Brace, the Nightsong resumes tonight. I'm going to go see her at the temple. Do yourself a favor and focus on the parts of your life Anathea doesn't touch. Remember who you were before the elf and remember you're still that person. Don't stop living the life you had before because your heart is sick with unrequited love. Count your blessings and be thankful. Don't be trapped in a fading moment."

The doors opened by themselves. Brace took the hint.

"I'll think it over. Promise."

"Do that. While you're at it, do make a list of the bars you feel are best in Spiral. We could go bar hopping when I get back from my little excursion. Oh, what drinking buddies we might be."

Brace nodded and showed himself out, shutting the doors behind him. He barely heard Tyr's words on the way out.

Tyr studied the inside of his mug and the trickle of beer that was left there. "Dear Anastasia," he said quietly, "If I could but sculpt words, I'd craft you a monument to tower into the sky. Countless books to scrape the heavens if set end to end in your honor. Would I could be an artist of any such guile."

What he was, however, was Tyr of the North, and he took comfort that in keeping with his friendship with her, that was enough.

The evening came and the Nightsong began. Once again, the

people of Spiral danced among the shimmerflies.

Anastasia and Tyr stood side by side, a pair of gods in human form, and watched from a balcony on the temple tower.

"Why are you leaving already?" Anastasia's eyes were narrowed at Tyr. "You've barely just woken up."

"I've got a bad feeling about the future. Not because of you. I think we need to start looking at other options to defend this city and this world. There's at least one more Sleeper out there and I think I know where to find them. I'm going to see if I can recruit some help."

"Let them sleep. The trouble's passed. Philosopher is off this world."

"Like you can trust him to stay gone. We're fools if we think the turmoil he started here magically ended here. It'll find other ways to express itself. It still stands to see how Spiral's surrounding kingdoms react to the presence of a goddess in their rival city."

Anastasia turned to put her hands on the rails. The wind stirred her hair and her loincloth. Even now, Tyr blushed to behold her, and behold her he did.

"I've had an idea about that myself," she said after a pause. "In Philosopher's favorite world there are honorable warriors known as Guildsmen. You know of them?"

"I did before I went to Sleep. Far stronger, faster and more agile than normal humans, with the ability to move along walls and ceilings. They regenerate their wounds."

"They're effective, to say the least of it. I'm going to create my own version of them here in Spiral from the ranks of the muses. My answer to his precious toy soldiers. I agree that Spiral's going to need protection well above the means of the city's guardsmen and below the level of what I'm going to try to accomplish." She brushed a thick strand of hair away and behind her ear. "I know violence is coming to Spiral. There's no stopping that."

"Then we both act in good conscience for the people of the city. By extension, the world."

Tyr took her shoulders in his hands gently from behind. The metal of his gauntlet felt cool against her right shoulder. "Ausarinia," he said in her ear, using her original mortal name. "You know I take you with me in my heart and mind wherever I go. I can travel to your side in a moment. You're not without me and I'm not without you. You know I'm not leaving you as such."

She put one hand over his metal clad fingers. "I just want my friends to feel closer to me than a world away right now."

"Ah, you should have just said so. I can wait a while before I leave."

Anastasia turned to him and smiled. "Tyr of the North, would you dance with me to the Nightsong?"

"Good lady, I'll dance with you on the coals of Hell if you but say the word."

He took her waist and clasped her hand. The rain began as they started to circle the balcony together, wetting them both and setting them laughing. Two friends loyal to each other for thousands of years danced together while the Nightsong played on.

"I question this city's adulation of Buron Hale at times. While he was a hero, he was also a darkened wreck of a man. He did the things he did because he was so violently robbed of his loved ones that he couldn't help being any other way. I knew a different kind of Buron, briefly, inside Gweldon's mountain. He was a good spirited man with a twinkle in his eye, an easy smile, and a sense of authenticity about him. I wish they'd known the Buron that I had known."

- Anathea's personal journals

Anathea had accepted charter at Spiral's largest hospital as a head nurse. It was soon evident that she was the authority on healing there, and it was said that inside a year she'd be running the place, top to bottom.

But tonight she sat in her room in Brace's house. Ander had moved in with Talais following the tumult of the city, leaving an open room that she quickly snatched up. Over the three months she had been there, she had also grown a tolerance to bean dip.

Brace was out at the temple with a muse tonight, no less. He was writing very well now that his self-confidence was recharged. She was proud of him, but had asked for the house to be hers alone for a couple of hours. He had conceded, knowing that Anastasia had given her a gift to be opened in private. She knew he still coveted her, but he understood to grant her distance now. She never promised him anything, but she was grateful for the friend he was turning out to be.

Anathea sat on her bed in her finest robes and broke the crystal.

Nothing.

Nothing.

Nothing.

She heard a plate fall over in the kitchen. "Don't tell me we have a rat," she spat, and hurried into the kitchen.

She stopped dead in her tracks, eyes wide.

Buron Hale had stood back up from knocking a plate over. He was eating a cookie. He offered her an extra in his hand "Cookie?"

Anathea stared. Tears ran down her cheeks. "Buron?"

"No less." He came around the counter. "First thing's first?"

She flew to him, threw her arms around him and held him tight.

"You're dead. You died. I saw you die."

"And you're a healer who doesn't make those mistakes. Yes, I'm dead. I'm only here for a bit. We were sort of cheated out of a reasonable goodbye, don't you think?"

She peppered his cheek with kisses. "I've never forgotten you. I've told people all about you. I've never let a day go by without thinking about you. I used to write you letters even though you were dead, when I was lonely."

"Why were you lonely? You went home, didn't you?"

"And I married Solan Vacht, the man I was pining for." She stepped back enough to look him in the eye and wiped hers clean of tears. "It was good for a time, but he was too materialistic. He didn't care for me any more than a trophy wife who'd had celebrity forced on her by a dragon."

"How long did it take you to sort that out?"

"Years. I kept trying to reach him and make him understand. I just couldn't. He cared about me, but he wasn't passionate about me. I was an afterthought to his political career when I wasn't helping him socially. I couldn't bear it anymore. I ran away from him and wandered the elven lands, and then through the human ones. And finally I came to Spiral. To be close to you and your memory."

He hugged her again. "I know you never forgot me. I'm thankful for that. I'm so sorry for Solan and all that noise back home. Of course, what's the first thing you did when you got here? Got straight into more trouble. Gods and goddesses, no less. You do overachieve on your drama."

She chuckled in spite of herself. "I just wanted to see what the city was like. Maybe walk the roads you did. I mean, you saved my life. You gave yourself up for me. I don't know if I've ever had a truer friend. All the people back home were so haughty and self-absorbed. I've truly known no one like you."

"So, come to the city I called my own to see if you could meet more Burons? I hope it didn't disappoint."

"I've been a bit off course on the matter, to be sure."

"That doesn't concern me. What concerns me is how far you've gone to run away from your past. It hurt you so badly that you left home to escape it and traveled across the world to this melodramatic mess someone had the bad taste to call a city. You're dragging weights and chains behind you with every footstep."

"I don't deny it. The streets of Spiral haven't lightened my burdens."

"And you won't lighten them yourself."

"How can I? I don't know how to get out from under it all. It haunts me by the minute."

Buron took her hands and stared into her eyes. "You took my past from me once. You felt guilty about it, remember? It's what made me who I was. When I remembered who I was, I was in pain, but I gave my life to save you. Not all teaching is without harm, and not all life lessons painless. That doesn't mean you can't become something more from learning from it."

"Wisdom is bought by tears, is that is?"

"It's the surest currency to buy it with, in my experience. I can't conjure out your past into a memory crystal and I see you haven't done it to yourself. Which means you understand the purpose of these burdens. You just haven't forgiven yourself for them."

Now, he cupped her face with hands. "I'm going to give you the gift you gave me without realizing it. Your past isn't important. Who you are, day by day, with every dawn, that's you. You remake yourself every morning when you get out of bed. You have a new chance every day to redirect everything. Every time the sun comes up you can let go of the day before and look to the day ahead."

He kissed her cheek and let his lips linger there. Then he said into her ear, "I release you from the past. You are absolved. Look only into who might be and how to be that person now. You are brilliant, Anathea, and you have brilliant friends now in Spiral. You have a life here. Go forward to it and stop blaming yourself for having feelings. Nobody's perfect. Just strive to go forward."

Anathea took his hands again and held them close to her heart. "I will. I promise. Hearing that from you makes it real. I understand."

"Only this time. You know I can't come back around again. The Muse felt you needed me one last time. She says you're a stubborn one."

Anathea laughed. "I suppose she would know."

He kissed her cheek again. "You were a precious friend in the time I knew you. I so desperately wish we'd have had more time. Just remember the time we had counted for much. Stand fast and be well. You can honor me best by being strong and never giving up your dreams."

"I promise. Thank you."

He stepped back and smiled. "I'm taking more of these cookies too, dammit. These are beyond amazing." he took three more, but they fell to the floor when he faded away. She heard him say, "Dammit."

She wondered in the times to come if it really had been Buron who came to her, or it was some magical dream.

In time she came to realize it didn't matter, because she did exactly what her friend advised her to do.

> "When I had forgotten how to love, I had forsaken how to live."
>
> - Calandros Pummet, the Great Poet of Spiral

Philosopher marched down the metal grate catwalks buried inside the hollowed out mountain known as Mount Seraphim. He was realities away from Anastasia now. He stalked up to his throne, the glowing blue sphere containing Anastasia's stolen power hovering over one hand.

He turned to sit down, and flung the sphere away. It spun into an alcove in the wall on the far side of the chamber. Other alcoves held other glowing spheres, each belonging to an Amaranthine he had imposed his will upon. All of them struggled with their playpen worlds now, much of their power stripped down and lacking the ability to shift between worlds or realities.

Then, his posture sank. He massaged his forehead with two fingers.

The Muse had spun his head around. Even in the clarity of his shadowy form, she had struck something soft. She had made him doubt.

No one else could have done so. He reasoned that she did it because her familiarity with him surpassed anyone else's, so naturally, she'd know exactly where to hit him. Surely, absorbing some of her undiminished power from that ridiculous quill had played a role, as well. It may have awakened in him the flawed humanity he had tried to banish.

And yet, her world might stand a chance. Maybe. Just maybe. She was more loving than any Amaranthine who had formed these worlds. She was more human than all of them. That was her greatest strength, yes. It won her the unconditional love of all the Amaranthines. It could win her the love of her own world.

He leaned back on his throne even further, looking upward at the cavern ceiling. Countless rock formations pointed down at him in silent accusation.

Her den realm, her private residence, was always so beautiful and warm.

This place was cold, empty, roughly hewn and dark.

"I belong here," he said to no one. *"I am the empty mountain."*

"That was your choice."

Philosopher stood up, senses alert. His pulse quickened. Nothing, but nothing was capable of sneaking up on him. The number of senses he wielded in his divine state made that impossible.

He cupped his right hand. Three silver barbs pierced his palm in a triangle formation. He walked across the grating leading up to his throne, eyes scanning the shadows.

"We've long feared that something of our power could manifest disastrous things subconsciously," the deep, even-toned voice told him. "You'd done it once in your last mortal life, realigning things to be closer to a mortal girl you favored. You've done it again now and you can thank the Muse for that."

Philosopher's eyes narrowed. He turned around.

Another Philosopher stood behind him, but all that was black was now colored in rich browns, and all that was silver was gleaming gold. He had a human complexion, his mane of long, silky brown hair was the same as his, and emerald green eyes stared at him with a mixture of pity and disappointment.

Philosopher flung his palm out, and three silver tendrils of razor wire snapped across the distance between them. They met only air and plunged into his throne in an explosion of rock.

A tendril of gold razor wire took his neck from behind in a

shining noose and threw him across the chamber, slamming him into the cavern wall. He found his enemy again as he stood up, with three gold razor wire streams receding into his palm, tipped with golden barbs.

"Don't look so surprised. You embraced the shadows again strictly because we think so differently at these opposite ends of our mental spectrum. I am precisely half of your total power, but you can't necessarily anticipate me."

Philosopher lunged again, a subhuman growl thundering in his throat. The lighter version of him disappeared again, but Philosopher launched his razor wire to the side, piercing his chest where he had rematerialized. He willed the barbs to curl and hold inside his enemy's flesh and jerked him forward. He grabbed this other Philosopher by the throat with his other hand, retracted his razor wire and punched him hard enough to shake the catwalk.

The other Philosopher shifted to a space just behind him and kicked. Philosopher felt the cavern wall again, but turned and leapt at other Philosopher with his wings giving one powerful flap to increase his speed.

Other Philosopher attempted to sidestep but couldn't move fast enough. Together they struck the far wall, where the shadowy Philosopher punched him in the face, breaking the cavern wall behind his enemy's skull.

Philosopher clasped other Philosopher's head in his hands and squeezed. *"Your weakness has fed the Great Enemy his greatest triumph yet. I defy your enfeeblement."*

Other Philosopher took his hands and pulled them apart, green eyes flaring. "It was my humanity the other Amaranthines loved us for. That's why we're alone now. You're incomplete and you know it."

Philosopher faltered. Other Philosopher head butted him, then kicked him away. Philosopher regained control mid flight and twisted to land on one of the catwalks beyond them.

"Why didn't you destroy Brace's feather? Or at least suck away its power like you have with most of the others of our kind?" Other Philosopher flapped his wings and coasted to the opposite side of the catwalk from his darkened self. "You were locked deep in shadow. You shouldn't have felt a thing."

"Touching the Muse's feather weakened me," Philosopher told him. He took a new stance and flapped his wings once, raising them like the hackles of a threatened cat. *"It clearly had something to do with you being here now."*

"It gave you what I needed to break free of the prison you trapped us in. Just as your poisonous thinking crept back into my mind, the Muse's feather sparked the doubt that crept into yours. Do you know what divorced us from each other at last? Self-loathing. The realization that this step we took to fight the enemy, embracing the darkness again, was the wrong choice!"

"It was the only choice!" Philosopher thundered. *"We searched for so many long years and for all of our power we found nothing. Nothing! They were depending on us to lead. We could not. We could not find any trace of an enemy we know to be out there, plotting and scheming against us all. What good is all of this power if we only use it to fail?"*

"I only realized recently, in the back of your mind, that this is what the Great Enemy wanted. He led us to this moment. He knew us intimately enough to see that if he merely denied us his existence, we would go mad with desperation and doubt. We would be reigning gods with no purpose between us, and he would simply have to wait until we came to this."

Other Philosopher reeled in his razor wire. "Look at me. I'm unwounded for all you've done. So are you. It is impossible for us to kill or even wound each other. Like I said, I have exactly fifty percent of the power you have, I have. We are divided evenly.

Everywhere except in our minds. We *can't* think precisely alike."

"You have no place in this world. You're an imitation of me, granted sentience against my will."

"What if I said the same for you right now? Can you tell which of us is the imitation? I can tell you one thing that separates us quite dramatically. It's the reason you didn't mute Anastasia's quill even after you found the power it had over you."

Philosopher's eyes narrowed. His wings lowered, but he remained silent.

"I am the side of you the Muse has loved for two thousand years, and you felt guilty for what you did to her. You tried to deny it, but it stayed and it festered. It turned you inside out eventually. You couldn't bring yourself to diminish the remaining sliver of her original perfection. You still can't. Instead, your soul convulsed and fashioned me. Or perhaps I shed you like a snake shedding skin and you're just the remnant of something tragic. Maybe you're sentient against my will."

Philosopher's pale hands balled into fists. *"What do you suggest? That I surrender myself to you? We recombine and you lead us into the same failures that poisoned us to start with?"*

"Precisely. At fifty percent of each we are still more powerful than any single Amaranthine, but now if they combined their efforts, they could destroy us. We no longer have absolute dominion over them. Not like this."

"Not with the powers I've stolen from them."

"When we recombine, I'll return their powers. Those that elect to follow us may do so. Those wounded enough by our hostility can stand aside if they wish it." Other Philosopher's eyes opened. "I only hope I can atone for all of this to Anastasia. You don't feel it there since I parted from you, but our love for her is the one thing that's ever redeemed us across the lonely millennia. If we've alienated her beyond our redemption, so be it, but we must try."

"I will not be brought to softness and distraction by her again." Philosopher walked toward other Philosopher, shadows gathering around him so only his fierce eyes were visible. *"Now I can operate without the smallest distraction. What you've done is erase that last of me that could be wounded by the lingering emotions in her quill. I am now perfectly mechanical in my mind. I can undertake the plans needed to stop the Great Enemy once and for all and never be brought low by* feeling."

Philosopher jumped at other Philosopher, who backhanded him away. Other Philosopher flew to the catwalk near the glowing spheres Philosopher used to store the stolen power of the Amaranthines. He reached for one, but a stream of razor wire constricted his wrist and pulled him backward. He right himself in mid air and landed before Philosopher, and the two engaged in a flurry of kicks, punches, elbow locks and throws that each managed to counter perfectly.

"Imagine your Muse in tears. Imagine the betrayal and suffering in her eyes. Think of how she looked to us on the streets of Spiral. Think of the betrayal in her eyes when we fought her in the skies and threw her down to the world without mercy. Think of your hands crushing her hope and engulfing Spiral in chaos. You cannot divorce yourself from your responsibility. Feel the destruction of her love for you anew and know that you deserve it."

Tears streamed from other Philosopher's eyes. He buckled, only for a moment.

Philosopher locked an arm around his throat from behind, twisted him away from the spheres, then held out a hand to summon their power. Streams of energy poured from the spheres and into his hand. His flesh glowed and his eyes smoldered. He pressed a hand against other Philosopher's chest with an exhale, mentally seized the power within his other self, and inhaled sharply, pulling his hand away.

Green energy crackled out of other Philosopher's chest.

"Now, you are merely forty nine percent," the shadow told him. He cupped a hand to other Philosopher's forehead and targeted a specific thread of knowledge in his mind, pulling it out in another crackle of green energy.

Philosopher towered above his wounded enemy now. He summoned the bulk of his power into one fist, which flared as brightly as a star, and slammed it into his other self. A blinding flash of light, and his other self was gone.

"I will not recombine with your weakness," Philosopher said, collapsing on the catwalk. He remained on all fours panting for several minutes as his power recalibrated itself. *"But I can cast you away through many realities, and steal your knowledge of the way back to me. Or Anastasia. Drift lost and forgotten forever."*

Philosopher got up and stumbled back to his throne. It would take time, but he would restore himself. He would be absent half of his power, but still he would be the architect of the Great Enemy's demise.

He sat smothered in his own darkness for a long, long, long time.

EPILOGUE

Brace Galter sat at his writing desk with the golden quill in his fingers and his head reclined over the edge of his wooden chair.

He had finally gotten the nerve to ask the Muse about the quill. He was still uncomfortable talking to her, and she had spent some time convincing him to think of her as a friend instead of a goddess. He was still trying to wrap his head around that.

She had told him, "You were never supposed to know it came from me. The best you might have assumed was that it was a magic feather of some kind, but not from me. Sorry about that. I saw you at the temple just before all of this started and I heard your plea. I wanted to do something to encourage you."

Having learned much about the Amaranthines' laws on a long talk with Tyr, he asked her, "So, you're fine with breaking these 'Amaranthine Laws' you've been so worried about?"

"Life isn't about rules, you know. It's knowing what the rules are so you know better when to break them," she said. "The other Amaranthines should really just leave me to it. Keep the quill, Brace. See what you can write with it. It'll make you feel inspired to write whenever you pick it up. That's the greatest gift it has."

He remembered the quill showing other impressive traits, too.

It had been a few months since the the great drama. Spiral had repaired itself as well as it could but the memory was still fresh. Some people walked the streets without meeting anyone's eyes. It was known that these were former rioters, but by the word of the Muse, they were left to deal with their own shame. Except for the ones who had committed murder. Those who didn't leave the city were outed by the goddess and taken to the King to be judged.

Brace barely saw Anathea anymore, even though she had moved in. He found himself adjusting to her on a more casual level. There were still moments when he pined for attention or had secret fantasies about her, but he knew these were his own concern now, and not something to trouble her with. She was warming to him over time, too, letting go and laughing more. The stoic elf, it seemed, really only wanted a sense of connection. She wanted a friend. He realized the blessing in being that person for her.

Of course, there was the matter of that particularly attractive muse at the temple, Leigh. They had talked long and she was teaching him gardening. Other times they would go to friendly dinners, where he was the envy of the men in the room to have her attentions. He found that she inspired him to write and write well. Tonight, he'd compose something strictly for her.

She was, in the end, a brilliant muse.

He studied the plaster patterns on the ceiling while shifting his chair side to side with his feet. He understood now his good luck. He had considered himself so low and unworthy before, so unremarkable and so beyond regard. Now he called not one but two divine beings as his friends (as Tyr vowed to take him bar hopping on his return). He was the friend and counsel of a beautiful elf who had become one of the greatest healers in Spiral. He had Leigh the muse, who kept him engaged and positive about the world regularly, not to mention keeping his creative tension spun tight. And of course, Ander and Talais visited twice a week on average.

The truth was, he had never felt more alive. He smiled frequently now and walked with his shoulders straight and his head high. People responded to that. He found it easier to be part of the world. He found he wanted to explode with words. He wanted to share everything with Spiral. Now that the restrictions about art were lifted by the Muse, his work could be known anywhere he wished to share it. A publisher was already interested in his words.

This is the time, he thought to himself. *This is the year to be alive. This is where our lives begin.*

He leaned forward and thought of his muse. The words would come easily now. They always would for her. All the same, he thought of everyone and felt humble. He felt unabashedly grateful.

For everyone then, he thought.

He dipped the golden quill into the inkwell on his desk and began to write.

Leigh, the girl formerly known as Princess Petrenella, finally felt at home.

She wore now the white silks of the muses of Spiral, and that freedom alone refreshed her. Yet it was the collection of books bestowed on her by her new sisters that delighted her most of all. Once they knew her tastes as a reader (and muses were very well read by nature of their business) they all donated books to her supply that they considered to be their personal treasures.

They were stacked around her room now, with her favorites beside her pillow as she slept. They pinned down the red velvet blanket and she had to move them out of her writing desk's chair if she wanted to sit down.

She had wept with the love that came with it. The muses accepted her readily and the very first night she was there, six of them sat with her and made her tell stories from the palace. They told her that she was a natural storyteller. While she asserted it was probably just an effect of having been a voracious reader, they told her that all the best writers were readers already.

They encouraged her to pick up a quill and try. Each muse had at least one pet art they practiced, and while Leigh showed enviable talent at gardening and animal care, she had never considered the calling of a wordsmith.

Oh, wouldn't her father have fits about that! Books were the most subversive things of all!

Try she did, of course. The more she wrote, the more she enjoyed it. The muses applauded her and gave her the best tips they could.

Sometimes, as she laid down to sleep, she'd let the books lie untouched at her sides and cry with happiness. Never had she felt more alive, never had she felt more loved and never had she felt so many tomorrows. She had a future. She tasted it. She wanted it. And it was a good future.

Tonight, she had let the books lie and dried the joyful tears with her blanket. Her fuzzymug, Lint, vaulted onto the bed.

He was the size of a softball and covered in soft, light brown fur. He had two large, adorable black eyes that seemed permanently innocent and no other features except a long, fluffy fur tail ringed with white.

He squeaked his love and nuzzled against her cheek, pressing into the hollow made by her head and her shoulder. He was asleep in a moment, eyes squeezed shut, trilling softly.

She stroked the back of his body and stared up at the deep red canopy of her four poster bed. *This is my Heaven,* she thought. *Long live the muses of Spiral.*

Other Philosopher awoke drifting in a black void. There was no light that he could see.

His body floated in a slow turn, wings pulled close around his body as his consciousness returned. The pain was gone, but he was still fatigued.

He could only do one thing against Philosopher's final attack. He realized his other self was stealing away his memories of how to cross realities and return. While he would still have the capacity to step through them from one reality to another, his enemy had sought to erase his memory of how to find his way to Anastasia or back to him. He had tried to erase those pathways from his mind.

Other Philosopher had focused all of his strength on hiding fragments of the whole deep in his mind, somewhere beyond the reach of Philosopher's attack. It had mostly worked. He might not know the exact way back to Spiral and to Anastasia's arms, but if he focused his will hard enough, he might remember enough to eventually return.

He crossed his wrists over his heart and laid his palms against his shoulders, and crossed his legs at the ankles. He kept his wings close, and shut his eyes. He began to explore himself in detail, fishing through memories for the threads he could use to rebuild the path back to her. The Muse came first. The Muse had to.

He wept from time to time, blue tears floating away into the darkness. He wept for his own madness and for the harm he had done to the greatest love he could ever have known.

Yet, that was the beacon for his way back. He anchored himself to his memories of Anastasia and pulled. He pulled as hard he could. He felt reality shift around him as he crossed from one to another, but still he found himself in a void.

It was going to be a long way out, if he could really find his way out at all.

I have to try. I have to put this right.

As he examined himself and his memories of her, free from the doubt that had first fueled his return to shadow, he realized he was no longer Philosopher. That could not be anymore. That was the soil from which he'd grown, but he was no longer that *thing*. He needed a renaming. Something in the very far distance of his memories said that names had power and importance.

Paragon, he decided. *I am the opposite of all the negativity of my other self. Paragon. I am Paragon.*

So named, he drifted in darkness, pulling on Anastasia with all of his strength, desperate to find his way home.

APPENDIX A:
THE POETRY OF BRACE GALTER

BOUNDLESS

This is not a cell.
This is a dream.
The walls have no meaning.
Simple swirls of plaster
containing untold secrets,
Revealed by the patient weaving
Of a boundless soul.
The flesh is weak.
Aging forward unto reaving
by time's insistence.
Book stacks form a ladder
And climbing up and reeling
From distant worlds revealed
In patient, waiting leaves,
I escape these boundaries seeming
To restrict the mind and heart
In mandate and law
and concrete rules of being.
Close my eyes and rest,

and I travel farther yet
over suns and moon laid gleaming
against a mental canvas,
through spiraling cities
and dense jungles steaming
as winter falls. My room
is a kingdom vast enough
to cradle me, awake or sleeping.

THE HOPE EATER

Dream-stripped eye awakens.
You stand there, flower dripping poison,
All subterfuge lays bare.
Silk hands that cut, smile that bites,
Voice that wracks and heart that denies.
Perfect shadows cover you
You give and pull away.
You love at your convenience.
You dismiss the wounds you cause.
Exalted by the eye
Coveted by flesh
Your soulless touch is a lie.
None know your subtle traps.
One by one to slaughter, come
To the angel eating hope.

CONQUEROR

Dancing.

Discreet.

Her smile hides behind a wineglass.

Lips breathing hot upon the glass....

An incidental mask.

Promises.

In every touch and laugh.

A glancing fingertip on the arm.

She shifts the weight on her feet.

A slight turn.

An obvious blush.

We're dancing

And only she knows the choreography.

Color.

A sunburst of life in a gray world.

Monochrome walls

Flank a glistening soul.

Enigma.

Layer upon layer hidden.

She keeps her secrets.

She laughs mine away.

A gentle glance.

An eyelash flutters.

We're dancing

And only she knows the motions.

She will not be conquered.

Conquerors seldom are.

DRIFTING

In the place where dreams collapse,
That nowhere place where the world meets the sky,
Dwells a woman, alone.
In this place of quiet nothings

She floats as if in water,
A slow spin with her feet off the ground.
And she wonders, "Is this what I am?"
But she has no answers.

There's nothing around to take judgment from.
Half heard voices and fading words,
People dissolved into memory
Before memory dissolves into time.

Her voice is quiet, for there are no ears
To listen to any protest.
No eyes to feast on her physical rapture,
No wit to regard her graceful turns,

No heart to share its empathy,
No arm to solace grant.
In this nowhere spin, she has these things
Yet finds her gifts denied release.

What is her point, spinning against the sky
And the place where the world meet?
She knows. She'll tell you this.
"My worth is that I am remembered

From before the world met the sky,
And in the memory of others
I'll have weight and measure again."
But she speaks it silently,

Muted only by human absence.
She will float and turn and float and turn
And anchor herself to human memory.
This is how a goddess must be.

WORLDS BEYOND

Of a hundred other worlds I've quiet dreamt,
Empires of splendored color against closed eye.
Sunbeams stealing dreams on break of cruel dawn.

None bears the cup of wonder more,
diluted in frequency and tedium;
all colors run gray, all magic forgotten.

Trapped within peaceless sleep and
the thieving rays of dawn-stolen dreams,
the world inside was dark as spent snow.

And so, all that was sleep was despair,
all the warmth of the inner world lost,
until she came forth, life an explosion around her.

With clever twist of rapier wit,
fall all cynical blades, disarmed, helpless,
and charm replaces cold at long last within.
Solely in the moment of herself, she erases despair.

A flicker of her eye, and the sun bears gifts,
rewarding the world with the dream of her heart
in lieu of kingdoms stolen by sleepy dawn;

and in the warmth of such disclosure,
even the dream-thieving rays of daylight
find themselves cherished and rendered forever innocent,

Their redemption bought by the glow of her glance.
Quickening the pulse, challenging the mind,
universes of potential framed in every look.

No eye bears jewels such as these.

So it is, the dark is calmed by a waking dream,
and wonder returns to the world in the cradle of her eyes.
A hundred kingdoms are scarcely worth the one within her mind.

APPENDIX B:
AFTERMATH OF THE FALLEN WING
(As written by Chronicler Ordeth Mahl)

On the subject of the Muse:

The Fall of the Muse, also known now as the Fallen Wing, shattered the peace of Spiral and remade the city into a form that the King himself all the way down to the lowest peasant was not prepared for.

The most obvious and dramatic effect of of these events was the revelation of a divine being overseeing our collective fate. Anastasia the Muse was considered a myth by many and a literally existing being by others, but having been cast down from the Heavens for all to see, there was no more room for deniability. Everyone had to confront that the Muse was real, and each had to reckon that knowing against their own powers of reason.

Some people fared better with this than others. The Mindful almost immediately revised their anti-Anastasia party line. Formerly, they declared that the suffering and pain of the world indicated that if Anastasia was real, she was a vain and aloof goddess at best, oblivious to the suffering of the mortal world. (Some have even suggested that she might rejoice in it). Therefore, because no reasonable person of such power would turn their backs on the suffering of the world, she must not exist.

Now that the Muse has actually walked up to them and looked some of them in the eyes, opinions changed. Anastasia told them that there were factors involved in her divine abstinence that precluded wantonly applying her power to the world. Some accepted this and came to a new understanding of Anastasia, converting to believers. Others took it as a poor excuse at best and still hold that the Muse is unworthy of worship or obedience in any way. If anything, they have become more militant about it.

Anastasia has declared that she holds free will sacred above all considerations, and that she will respect their point of view. She made some comment about peaches and people disliking them, but it seems not to have sunk in with her audience. Seeing that they will not be punished by Anastasia even though they dismiss her, the Mindful have returned to vocally attacking her every move, seeing it as further proof of her decadence. What opinion Anastasia has about this behavior remains behind closed doors.

On the subject of the Mindful after this event:

It is known that much violence was directed at the known Mindful during the riots, naturally by true believers who had convinced themselves that only weeding out the impure among them would restore Anastasia to the Heavens where she belonged. Surprisingly, the Muse has been very strict in dealing with those believers who she was able to identify as acting criminals (something she has shown incredible precision in doing). Some were banned from Spiral and her sight, and others were given stern reprimands. Others were directed to hundreds of hours of community service.

As one might expect, the faithful went about these tasks without protest, even with some eagerness, which seemed to unnerve the Muse considerably.

On the subject of the riots and their cost:

In terms of the violence itself, only the King knows how many were killed or injured, or what the damage tallies up to in ring-coins. There are many rumors about why the King refuses to release this information. His own word goes that he wants to promote healing in

Spiral, and that he wishes the people to look forward to a new dawn and not obsess over the wounds inflicted by the riots.

Many believe that the numbers are high enough that the people will question his use as a King. After all, the Goddess herself walks among us now, and daily there are those who clearly announce their fealty to her above the King. This would not sit will with most Kings and it is said Ronmacharte is no exception. Whispers go about that the court of the King feels a tremendous loss of power with the Muse's influence in the city waxing. It's also said that the King fears to do anything more about this than whisper.

That being said, I personally suspect that the King is hesitant to confront Anastasia on his fears of another Raven Muse. The actions of a renegade muse named Senelle just over a century ago are surely not forgotten by the King, as it remains one of the most popular tragedies in Spiral.

To revisit, Senelle was a muse of the temple who believed pain was more instructional than inspiration. She was a cunning manipulator who enticed many artists into thinking not only well with her, but into falling in love with her. Then she would break their hearts in any number of ways: cutting them off completely with no communication, emotional abuse, flights of rage over seemingly trivial things, or publicly shaming them.

While she did accrue much in the way of tortured art (the quality of which is entirely subjective and is better left explored in another writing), she pushed two of her artists to suicide. One of them was the youngest son of an earlier King Ronmacharte.

Oh, what must be going through the head of the King now. The King may fear that Anastasia might release a flock of Raven Muses as a secret weapon if he displeases her, strategically pointing them at "soft targets" that can damage his power. Politicians and lackeys all can be swayed by the right muse, after all. An urban legend has persisted in Spiral for decades that Raven Muses exist in the shadows, but if they were real, we surely would have heard accounts of them by now in our assessments of the riots.

On the directive to liberate art from Anastasia:

Meanwhile, the King has obeyed Anastasia's directive to free the art stored in the city's vaults. This we know he did through grit teeth, as his face was flushed a color of red and then purple at the news. This we have from the Muses themselves, who were on hand to deliver the message. Art is flourishing in Spiral like it hasn't since before Thurach came. The people are excitedly talking about their favorite books in cafes now, classics long buried beneath the King's feet. Galleries are showing exclusive "lost works" freed from the darkness of the vaults, and they are selling at a brisk pace. Theaters, and those operated by the Blue Children in particular, have seized upon reams of plays, and wasted no time acquiring funding from curious patrons to produce them.

To the delight of the Muse herself, it's said, poetry is whispered in the streets and alleys of Spiral. Each verse is a secret laid bare in the shadows, and many youths are actually paying shadowy figures to recite "the Stolen Verses" long held under lock and key. This they take home to their lovers and friends and not so much recite as perform, seeing the language take on a dimension long oppressed by the King's fears.

Spiral was always said to be the "Creator's City," insofar as this city's emphasis on art applies. You can't turn a corner in Spiral without an intricate mural, meticulously crafted sculpture or street choir greeting you. The release of art's finest work into the city streets has had a telling effect. The people who were rioting before now hurriedly devour old books they've never seen and discuss unknown sculptures of grandiose work that are being mounted all over the city.

We will have to see how the wounds of the riot affect the art and expression of the people here on in. We must not forget that a literal goddess of art resides here openly now, and that will magnetize artisans from all over the world to come here. We should prepare for a major boom in tourism.

On the matter of Creative Magic and Formulaic Magic:

Most tellingly, new magic is blossoming in the streets. Creative Magic has been unleashed and it is a very different animal from Formulaic Magic. Formulaic Magic has been defined now as the math that maintains the world and provides structure to the status quo by being dependable, consistent and accessible to anyone with magical potential the same way.

Creative Magic, we know now, is unleashed by those of magical potential who are consumed by the arts. It drives them almost the point of madness, it seems, goading them to create and express to the exclusion of any other considerations. Creative Mage seize upon an art or three that calls to them and the more they explore it, the more they unlock their potential, so expression is the cornerstone of their craft.

This magic, however, takes many personalized forms. They always suit the personality and outlook of the individual creator and sometimes they even have to perform their craft to enact it. From there it can have variable levels of power based on their practice, but it is known that one must explore himself or herself in soul searching ways to advance this potential further. It can produce effects similar to Formulaic Magic without duplicating the attention to Arcane Formulae (something it's said the King's wizard, Cappus, is most unnerved by). It can create designs in the universe unknown before the imagination of the Creative Mage took form.

In other words, Formulaic Magic can be used to raise and nurture hundreds of roses, but only Creative Magic can create a kind of rose no one has ever seen before.

As one would expect, consuming the highest quality of art around them helps Creative Mages as well. They are half devoured by their passion to create, and half divine for empowering it.

On the possibility of a "new breed" of muses:

As if all of this was not worth heavy consideration by itself, Anastasia has been taking a new interest in the training of her muses. Formerly, the muses were little more than traveling priests and priestesses, by our reckoning. They would wander far and wide, through the city and the world as a whole, seeking to inspire the next great work of art. The have alternately been counselors, mediators and pillars of the community in a general sense. In fact, the muses are so integral to atmosphere of this city that I suggest the morale of the people would plunge if they were to disappear overnight.

One must take a moment to appreciate what the muses bring to the table. They tend to be educated, well read and trained to be experts in the study and creation of art. Sometimes, multiple forms of art. They are taught diplomacy and communication, and psychological study. They are trained to be extroverts, gregarious and approachable to everyone they meet. All of this, the better to seek out potential creators and fuel them with the passion to create something magnificent.

They are also, it is known, trained to fight. A long staff is the favored weapon of the muse, but defense of the temple usually mandates a sword and shield. They are taught basic healing remedies. No muse leaves the temple without the ability to defend herself, often with her bare hands, against multiple attackers. To be clear, they are not soldiers or meant to be soldiers, and they avoid killing at almost all costs. They will absolutely defend themselves if attacked, whether it's a gang of ill-intended rioters or someone who would dare manhandle them.

It's this latter set of qualities Anastasia is looking to boost. There are rumors in the temple that a new type of muse altogether is being crafted, one with martial leanings. To our surprise, she is not focusing on men for this role. Being that only nine percent of the muses are male, we had figured this would give them greater utility. Instead, it seems Anastasia is focusing this effort entirely on her female muses.

Most interesting of this news: It seems these new martial muses are showing special powers. This is doubtless some innate magic, and I personally suspect she's tapping into the surge of Creative Magic. That's as far as we know things to be. Are they being trained to have a set series of talents and magical endowments (IE, via Formulaic Magic, which is logical) or are they being trained individually in powers personalized to each one (Creative Magic?) Surely, she couldn't be mixing the two.

What she plans with these muses, we do not yet know. In this matter in particular, Anastasia has not been forthcoming. It's been suggested that given her flair for the dramatic, as all artists are known to suffer from, she will likely give them a new name and a new look. Will our white silk clad muses soon be joined by a kind of muse we'd not recognize altogether? Time may tell. The Muse will not.

All of this creates an interesting system of consequences, a chain of events that must inevitably unfold. We are making projections about the future, but with the Muse as a wild card in the equation, our figures are uncertain. We can only wait and see how these recent events shape the future of Spiral.

APPENDIX C:
THE LAWS OF THE MUSE
(Traditionally declared to be the words of Anastasia herself, now annotated by the goddess following the Fallen Wing.)

"You belong to no one. No one belongs to you. You are a force of nature and a spirit of creativity, a soul devoted to the power of human expression. Embrace everyone."

Look, I don't mind if you have your loves and if you didn't feel attraction, chances are you couldn't be as effective a muse. I'm flexible on this one. I would never deny my muses true love, but I hope they learn enough about love and attraction to be certain of what they have when they find it. There is no greater pain for the world than a muse with a broken heart.

"Your dignity and pride may be defended freely and always without reprimand."

I fully authorize and encourage you all to fight well and with competence. Master whatever weapons you choose. If you are attacked, defend yourselves, and others if you must. While it's my preference that you do not kill, I will look the other way if your life is on the line. You are not toys to be broken at the whims of others.

"A muse can only ever be touched by her own consent, no matter what the circumstances. The muse alone decides this."

I'm surprised sometimes that I had to make this a rule. No one is entitled to your personal space and no one is entitled to manhandle you for any reason. Consent is the most important virtue here, and you have full control of it, obligation free to any admirer. Consider law number 2 to be in effect if someone even lays a hand on you without your permission, minus the obvious part about killing.

"Revel in the arts. You may linger on a favorite type but sample everything. Inspire in the fields you know best."

I want my muses to be well schooled in all forms of art, but I encourage you to adopt the arts that speak most to you. If you love sculpting, take audience with other sculptors. If you love acting, find other actors and actresses. You can learn from each other as you inspire them, and you should never expect that your learning is ever done. Consider every artist you meet a kindred spirit and do what you can to engage their creative powers, but by all means, nurse your own passions too.

"A muse may decide where she is best needed, and she may roam and explore freely the world as she chooses."

There are two ways that artistic minds can find us. They can come to the temple and apply for the personal counsel of a muse, or we go out into the world and find local creators and prompt them to be brilliant. You may choose which you want to do and you can change your mind at any time. You are also not beholden to problematic artists, and you may disengage from that at will, for whatever reason you elect, but I do prefer you have a solid reason to do so and not to pursue idly whimsy here. Also, just between us, this is me giving you license to get away from toxic/clingy people - artists or otherwise - if things somehow get out of hand with them. Refer again to law number 1.

"A muse should not compare herself to others, and should encourage others to do the same."

A wise old friend I only partially knew I had told me this before he died, and it's always been good advice. Please, don't compare yourself to others. You may never be satisfied with your work or your stylistic choices. It's good to have your heroes, but remember that striving for craftsmanship is the ultimate journey. Don't let the works of others, especially rivals, intimidate you. Go forward with conviction and create what you love, according to how you want to create it, and believe. Put your attention on how you want your feelings to be expressed, not on the envy of others.

"Find the beauty in the world wherever it dwells and immortalize it in your own way."

This plays into what I said for law number 6. Your view is worthy. Your direction is yours to determine. Your art answers to your judgment. There is so much to be loved in the world, yes, even in a dark world. There is beauty that must be captured and conveyed to the people. Your responsibility is to encapsulate emotion and present it to others. I would have it that you remind the world that having feelings is a worthy and noble thing, but darker works of warning against the perils of a callous soul are equally important. You are to resonate the strength and majesty of the world around you. Embrace it.

"Defend art and beauty wherever it is threatened. You may use any means necessary as this preserves the very fabric of civilization."

A work of art has no definitive lifespan. It may or may not be timely, but the execution will be a lesson for other minds long after the life of the craftsman. It will resonate with the people when the age that spawned it is beyond living memory. Therefore, art IS the fabric of civilization. It is vital to the progress and maintenance of a culture. Defend any threatened expression as passionately as you can. Enlist whatever aid you wish, but do the very best you are able to ensure that creative works are protected from harm. Consider this one of our most sacred tenets.

"Never use your powers of inspiration for your own selfish gains."

Never forget the selfish workings of the Raven Muse. You are human, and your flawed, and I accept this more readily than you know, but calculated ruthlessness will result in being expelled from the order and banned from any temple where my name is even whispered in a corner. Do not destroy others for glee or comfort. I forbid this.

"Never restrain your passions. Be free in thought and feeling. Let your fellow muses be your counsel."

You should never feel like you have to hide what you're feeling from the world, especially from your fellow muses. Declare yourself as openly as you choose, but don't let anything stay you when you have something relevant to say. Share yourself with the world in the quantities you feel comfortable with (even if that changes day to day), but share yourself. My muses should never be described as a secretive and unreadable lot. Part of your greatest power is your honesty. Wear your emotions on your sleeve and let them blossom unrestrained: This alone can inspire dozens.

APPENDIX D:
RUMORS AND URBAN LEGENDS OF SPIRAL
(Annotated by Leigh Veeh)

1) At the center of Spiral lays a great secret, kept from the people by the ruling family from time out of mind. This is said to be: Immortality, enlightenment, the gateway to another world, perpetual youth, the secret history of the world, or the Goddess Anasasia herself. *(With Anastasia having revealed herself to us, this last one seems unlikely).*
2) The graveyards of spiral, located in vast underground chambers lit by glowmoss and glittertrees, see the dead rise from the grave every night to pantomime what they remember of their living days until they return to their rest or fall apart. This is why no one is allowed in the Undercrypts after dark.
3) A vast complex lies beneath Spiral, an undercity that mirrors the above but filled with inhuman creatures and forgotten horrors. Spiral was built to imprison them. *(This does not strike me as likely, given the massive undertaking that building the Tubes represented. Nobody I know of reported eldritch horrors during their construction).*
4) Anastasia is pushing for public nudity to steal men away from their wives! *(This one is laughably obvious. Clearly started by threatened housewives. I'll note that Anastasia has pointed out that there are no laws banning public nudity of any kind in Spiral as it stands, but she also points out that her muses are capable of fighting very, very well in the same breath. Not that they need to with a goddess watching over them.*
5) The city of Spiral was built to honor a woman named Ora, of whom almost nothing is known. It's said her grave rests at the heart of Spiral and is only visited by nobles. *(This might have fit in with the first entry above, but I liked it enough to*

keep it separate).

6) No one knows why Thurach attacked Spiral, and to this day conjecture continues toward his motivation. Some say he sought the secrets at the heart of Spiral, while others say he was invited to attack by the ruling family to bolster their power among the people in the aftermath. Rumors of Thurach one day returning in force are common.
7) Anastasia the Muse has a darkened aspect dedicated to violence, chaos and despair. This aspect has separated itself from her and acts against her in all things. *(Anastasia has denied this wholeheartedly).*
8) The God of Dragons (alternately, their progenitor or an eldest member of their race) sleeps deep beneath Spiral within a vault of secret knowledge. Variation of this suggests it is a prisoner instead. *(Must ask Anastasia about this, but seems unlikely).*
9) The Muse's heart breaks whenever an artist turns away from a path of creation. *(She has said nothing to this effect either way, but she is still new to us).*

Made in the USA
Lexington, KY
20 June 2017